"Wake up! Come on, open your eyes!"

With a groan, Josh obeyed. Through the opening in the windshield, he saw a light. A face appeared, floating in the light. A beautiful face. Soft glowing skin, a wide luscious mouth, huge greenish eyes. Surrounded by a fuzzy, burnished halo. An angel.

"Can you move? Then do it!"

Bossy angel, Josh thought. He heaved himself through the windshield. A small angelic hand grabbed to help him. Eventually he lay on rough, wet rock. His rescuer sat beside him, breathing raggedly.

Breathing. Not an angel, then. Real...

And pregnant!

Dear Reader,

March roars in like a lion at Silhouette Romance, starting with popular author Susan Meier and *Husband from 9 to 5*, her exciting contribution to LOVING THE BOSS, a six-book series in which office romance leads to happily-ever-after. In this sparkling story, a bump on the head has a boss-loving woman believing she's married to the man of her dreams....

In March 1998, beloved author Diana Palmer launched VIRGIN BRIDES. This month, *Callaghan's Bride* not only marks the anniversary of this special Romance promotion, but it continues her wildly successful LONG, TALL TEXANS series! As a rule, hard-edged, hard-bodied Callaghan Hart distrusted sweet, virginal, starry-eyed young ladies. But ranch cook Tess Brady had this cowboy hankerin' to break all his rules.

Judy Christenberry's LUCKY CHARM SISTERS miniseries resumes with a warm, emotional pretend engagement story that might just lead to *A Ring for Cinderella*. When a jaded attorney delivers a very pregnant stranger's baby, he starts a journey toward healing...and making this woman his *Texas Bride*, the heartwarming new novel by Kate Thomas. In *Soldier and the Society Girl* by Vivian Leiber, the month's HE'S MY HERO selection, sparks fly when a true-blue, true-grit American hero requires the protocol services of a refined blue blood. A lone-wolf lawman meets his match in an indomitable schoolteacher—and her moonshining granny—in Gayle Kaye's *Sheriff Takes a Bride*, part of FAMILY MATTERS.

Enjoy this month's fantastic offerings, and make sure to return each and every month to Silhouette Romance!

Mary-Theresa Hussey

Mary-Theresa Hussey
Senior Editor, Silhouette Romance

Please address questions and book requests to:
Silhouette Reader Service
U.S.: 3010 Walden Ave., P.O. Box 1325, Buffalo, NY 14269
Canadian: P.O. Box 609, Fort Erie, Ont. L2A 5X3

TEXAS BRIDE

Kate Thomas

Silhouette
R O M A N C E™
Published by Silhouette Books
America's Publisher of Contemporary Romance

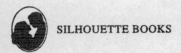

For my parents—
whose love of reading was the source.

SILHOUETTE BOOKS

ISBN 0-373-19357-2

TEXAS BRIDE

This edition published by arrangement with Harlequin Books S.A.

® and TM are trademarks of Harlequin Books S.A., used under license. Trademarks indicated with ® are registered in the United States Patent and Trademark Office, the Canadian Trade Marks Office and in other countries.

Printed in U.S.A.

KATE THOMAS

As a navy brat, Kate moved frequently until she was lucky enough to attend college in Texas. She married a native Texan, produced another and remained fascinated by language and cultural diversity. With her writing, she likes to celebrate one trait that all humans share: a desire to love and be loved.

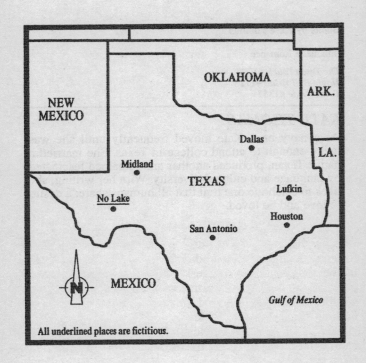

OKLAHOMA

ARK.

NEW
MEXICO

LA.

Dallas

Midland

TEXAS

Lufkin

No Lake

Houston

San Antonio

N

MEXICO

Gulf of Mexico

All underlined places are fictitious.

Chapter One

As he slid another CD into the car's player, Josh Walker frowned. Damned if he'd admit it, but—he was lost. Smack in the middle of the biggest nothing he'd ever seen. No trees, no houses, no other traffic. Aside from some stubby wildflowers edging the road, this western half of Texas held nothing but cactus and rocks.

And weather, Josh amended. The blue-black clouds that had begun piling up along the horizon just an hour ago now filled the sky.

Josh swore. He'd encountered one—count 'em, one—intersection since leaving the interstate and he must have made the wrong turn. Dammit, he should be in San Angelo by now.

Not that it really mattered. The case in Midland had wrapped up unexpectedly this morning when his client accepted a new settlement offer. Josh had called his office back in Virginia, but there was nothing pressing at the moment.

So he'd packed away his suit and tie, donned jeans and a well-washed chambray shirt—and the boots he still favored over athletic shoes, even after years of living back East—and climbed into his outrageously expensive imported car to indulge in the one pleasure he could always count on: a long, solitary road trip. Ordinarily, the silent slipping of miles beneath the wheels relaxed him and chased the stress from his mind.

Only it wasn't working this time. Hell, nothing was working these days. His work no longer absorbed him; his house was just an investment; even sex— The last careful, casual physical relationship had left him completely cold. Dissatisfied. *Empty.*

Damned if he'd admit *that,* either. He was only twenty-nine. His life was not empty. Everything was fine.

Josh growled at the bright, cheerful April wildflowers dancing in the wind. Well, okay. Maybe his life was a little sterile, predictable and lonely, but— *No, not lonely.*

Solitary. By choice.

Because that was the only safe choice. He'd learned that lesson six years ago in earth-shattering fashion, when his girlfriend had disappeared for a weekend. To get rid of his baby. Without asking him. Without even bothering to *tell* him. If it hadn't been for that blabbermouth friend of hers, he might never have discovered the truth.

But he had. For a day or two, anguish and anger had threatened to devastate him.

Then he'd fought back. Slammed a permanent lid on useless emotion. Stayed busy.

It had worked, too. He'd finished first in his class in law school. Built a successful practice, specializing in environmental issues. And he'd never been hurt by a woman again. Therefore, even though he'd been a little...*restless* lately, he still thought he was perfectly happy.

Certain other people disagreed. His secretary, Marletta, was making retirement noises, even though she was only forty-eight. And his sister-in-law—

Josh snorted softly at the way Matt's wife had taken his

inventory last month when he'd gone back to Montana to attend his newest nephew's christening. When his younger brother, Dan, showed up with Mei Li, his new Amerasian bride, Annie had teased Josh about being the last unmarried Walker. Told him he'd better get moving.

He'd snarled back that hell would freeze over before he'd get involved with a woman again—and stalked out of the house.

Annie had strolled outside after him, folded her arms on the top rail of the corral and calmly asked him when he was going to stop feeling sorry for himself.

It wasn't self-pity, he'd protested. It was wisdom won the hard way.

As he put the car through a curve, Josh shook his head, recalling how Annie had just steamrolled on. *You don't hold the patent on being hurt, Josh. Everybody gets wounded. It's part of living. If you want to suffer, that's your choice. But if you want to heal—stop picking at the scab!*

The best way to do that is to find someone who's hurt worse than you are and help them.

Nonsense, of course. But somehow Annie's words had stuck in his head. Even now, weeks later, he couldn't seem to forget them.

He didn't understand what her suggestion was supposed to accomplish, though. Was he supposed to feel smug and self-satisfied for doing a good turn? Or grateful because he was so much better off by comparison?

Besides, Josh thought as the rumble of thunder drowned the CD's music, he didn't know anyone who'd been hurt worse than he had....

As the old pickup coasted to a stop, Dani Caldwell guided it toward the edge of the pavement. Unless she missed her guess, the truck had thrown a rod, which meant...

Dani swallowed the panic rising through her, since there

was no point to it. The disaster had already happened; now she just had to pick up the pieces and move on.

"I should be getting good at this," she muttered as she collected the small sack of groceries she'd spent her nearly-last dollar on, then clambered awkwardly down from the pickup cab. "I'm sure getting enough practice! Maybe that's what I'll do after the baby comes—give seminars in coping."

To keep her mind occupied with something besides the stifling afternoon heat, her crippled finances, the terminally ill truck or her *real* problems, Dani elaborated on the silly theme as she trudged down the narrow, seldom-used state road toward the primitive cabin that was now both refuge and prison.

"I'll start small, with free lectures to church groups. Then hotel ballrooms at a fee. In no time at all, I'll be the Queen of Coping, with infomercials, books, videos—"

Her foot slipped on a stone and she had to fight to stay upright. That might do it, Dani conceded as she shifted the groceries to the other arm and continued on. So far, she'd fought her difficulties to a standstill, but a broken ankle—out here in the middle of West Texas Nowhere—might actually convince her to give up.

But her ankle wasn't broken, she reminded herself firmly. And she was young, strong and determined. *Also broke, widowed, pregnant and just about job skill-less....*

The baby kicked her so hard she staggered. Dani grinned and patted her bulging abdomen. "That's your first comment today," she said, "and you're right, tiger. No self-pity. We'll figure something out. Besides, we're almost home." Just before the next dry streambed, she turned off the road at the odd half-palm, half-yucca tree. It marked the beginning of the narrow rocky path that followed the wash for a few yards, then curved around a big boulder before rising to her latest hiding place, a one-room hunting cabin that belonged to a schoolmate's uncle.

Dani had to pause to rest at the boulder. The book said that tiring easily was natural so close to delivery.

"Just a couple more weeks, darling," she whispered to the precious burden she carried beneath her heart. "Then we'll begin our new life together." As she rested, Dani stared out over the stark desert landscape, so unlike the lush Piney Woods of East Texas where she'd grown up.

A wave of homesickness swept over her and she allowed herself one minute for wishing things were different. For wishing she could have stayed in Lufkin to have her baby.

For wishing her baby could have known its father.

Dani closed her eyes, but the pain she'd once felt over Jimmy's death had faded to weary acceptance in the six months since he'd caught a bullet meant for one of his hot-headed barroom buddies. When the doctors declared him legally dead the next day, the very last of her hopes and illusions had died too.

And she'd had so many! She'd fallen in love at first sight—the instant she'd bumped into Jimmy Caldwell while filing into the high school cafeteria for freshman orientation. Within weeks they'd been going together, and four years later, on her eighteenth birthday, she'd married him and settled down to live happily ever after.

Dani sighed. "Ever after" had turned out to be five years. As for the happily part, well... They'd been happy for a while, but Jimmy had changed so much—especially in the last two years—that by the time he'd disappeared into the night that final time, the boy she'd loved had become a complete stranger.

"But don't worry, baby. I won't make the same mistake twice." Dani didn't have time to nurse another broken heart; she had a baby to bring into the world and raise.

Oh, she wasn't naive enough to think that doing it alone would be easy, but she had no choice and that at least made it simple.

No choice. Dani smoothed her hand over the baby. Her

parents were gone, killed in a car wreck only weeks after her wedding. And Jimmy's folks... Dani held them largely responsible for her husband's unhappiness and self-destructive behavior. They'd pressured him relentlessly to be the first, the best, the most. When he couldn't measure up, he'd sought comfort with casual drinking companions instead of his wife.

Well, they weren't getting a chance to damage her child with their heavy-handed treatment.

Unfortunately, her in-laws had different ideas. They also had money, powerful contacts throughout the state, and no qualms about using any means necessary to get what they wanted.

And what they wanted—now that their only son was dead—was sole custody of their grandchild. Dani refused to give up her child, but she had no resources to fight them.

So she'd run. And run. And run again.

She'd planned to wait out the last of the waiting here, then head for a good-size town and use her tiny emergency fund to pay for a midwife and a night or two in a cheap motel. After the due date, she was going to clean houses or baby-sit while she worked out the details of a real career path.

"So much for plans," she muttered. The truck breaking down had *not* been in her scenario. Now what?

A deep rumbling made her look up. Dark clouds filled the sky, flashing streaks of lightning over the desert like party streamers.

"Thank you." Dani addressed the thunderheads with a little laugh. "I was just about to waste my time worrying—as if that ever created a solution."

The first, chilly raindrops splattered the dust around her. "I do have a roof to put over us," Dani told her unborn child, pushing off from the rough limestone and resettling the grocery sack. "And I think I'd better hurry up and do it!"

As she hustled up the path, making it through the cabin door just before the rain started in earnest, Dani welcomed the distraction of the storm. She tried to think positively for the baby's sake, but she didn't honestly know how much longer she could keep up her brave front.

With no car, no job, no money, alone and a baby coming...

"Oh, stop whining," she ordered herself. "Lots of people are worse off than you are." Smoothing her hand over her baby's current address comforted Dani, as usual. "I don't know how we'll manage, but we will," she promised the son or daughter who was kicking merrily against her rib cage. "Because no matter what—I *won't* give you up."

While the storm grew in intensity, Dani kept herself busy mixing up corn bread and doctoring black-eyed peas to make Texas caviar.

Biting back a swearword, Josh fought to keep the car on the road as downdrafts from the thunderstorm buffeted it. Then the rain hit—the fat, individual drops splatting on his windshield quickly became a deluge his wipers could barely handle.

Josh pressed on the gas pedal, eager to drive out of the storm, find a town and check into a motel. He was tired. He'd had enough of the desert. *Enough of being lost.*

When the rain thickened into a solid curtain, he slowed a little.

An inch or so of water covered the road in a few spots. The car hydroplaned across them, but the tires regained their traction almost immediately. He relaxed against the leather upholstery.

Suddenly a dark shape loomed in front of him and Josh swerved just in time to avoid sideswiping it. A truck, he realized as it disappeared into the grayness again. Some damn fool hadn't pulled completely off the pavement.

Just ahead, another shallow layer of water stretched from one side of the pavement to the other.

At least he wasn't the only person ever to drive down this road. Which meant it went somewhere, too. With a sense of relief he refused to acknowledge, Josh increased his speed.

And drove right into hell.

The nose of Josh's car hit the edge of the water; forward momentum carried the rest of the vehicle into the torrent before his foot could hit the brakes. Like a greedy child snatching up a toy, the angry current grabbed the car, pulled it off the side of the road, then spun it—once, twice, three times—slamming Josh's head against the doorpost with each furious revolution.

One more shuddering impact with something and the car came to a halt.

Josh managed to unfasten the seat belt, but the churning torrent held the door shut against his dazed efforts to open it. The electric window controls didn't work. He tried the passenger door, but it was jammed shut, too.

Before his head cleared enough to think straight, a large piece of debris smashed into the car. The impact sent Josh bouncing off the steering wheel into the doorpost again, then rammed his head into the dash. Stars exploded behind his eyes.

Through the haze of pain disorienting him, Josh noted water seeping into the car, filling the floorboards, rising.

He was going to drown here. In this gritty, muddy water. As consciousness faded despite his efforts to stay alert, Josh tasted real regret. *Maybe my life is empty,* he thought, *but...I don't want to die!*

The oven baking the corn bread threatened to toast Dani, too, so she went out on the porch to breathe some rain-cooled air.

She was about to step back inside when an odd sound

came thinly through the storm. It took her a moment to recognize... Then she was struggling into a jacket and scrambling for the flashlight and turning back for the length of old rope she wouldn't trust to hold a cat's weight. It was all she had.

"That sounded like metal, baby. Like a car being hit! If someone's in trouble, we can't turn our back on them, so hang on," she said, finding a way, despite her loaded-down arms, to pat her stomach encouragingly. "Hang on!" she yelled into the misty gloom. Thank heaven, the rain seemed to be slowing.

As carefully but as quickly as possible, Dani slid down the path to the big boulder, then scrambled past it to peer at— *Oh, God. It* was *a car. In the creek.* Caught for the moment against her boulder's twin out in midstream.

The furious, foaming runoff was trying to pull it away from the rock and drag it downstream. If she was going to rescue the passengers, she'd have to act quickly.

Maybe there isn't anyone inside. Dani grasped at the possibility. Maybe they'd gotten out. Maybe the car had broken down—like her truck—and been abandoned. Maybe she didn't have to risk the baby....

Biting her lip, Dani aimed the flashlight beam at the vehicle. A dark human shape slumped over the steering wheel.

"Well, that makes it simple," she muttered, tucking the flashlight into her windbreaker. She tied one end of the rope around the yucca tree and the other end under her breasts, took a deep breath and waded into the torrent.

Letting the rough current push her toward and around the rear of the car, Dani grabbed for and found a handhold on the midstream boulder. After crawling awkwardly to its top, she inched along it, wiping the now-occasional raindrop from her eyes. And babbling, she realized as she reached a spot near the front of the car. That idiot pleading and praying aloud was her.

Okay. God probably has the idea. Now do your part.

Pulling out the flashlight, Dani pointed it at the still figure in the car. The ray of light showed only a few details clearly: the gleam of dark gold hair, a firm jaw, and broad, unmistakably male shoulders. His eyes were closed, but... Dani steadied the shaking beam and peered through the raindrops beading the windshield. Yes, the man's chest moved. He was unconscious, but alive.

Dani's sigh of thanksgiving became a groan as the flashlight revealed another problem. There was water inside the vehicle, already lapping over the console. Clamping her jaws together, Dani put away the flashlight. The man in the car was going to die unless she did something. Now.

The top of the boulder was littered with loose rocks. Picking up the biggest one, Dani lifted it over her head, aimed it at the windshield and let fly. She repeated the process until the glass starred, then heaved the rock one more time. As the spray of safety-glass nuggets subsided, Dani leaned down and peered through the opening she'd created to get a better look at the man she was trying to rescue.

Heat coiled deep inside her. Completely inappropriate reaction, she told herself. But just as completely undeniable.

Okay, so cope with it. And get back to work.

Despite her urgency, Dani couldn't help studying the man for a few long seconds. He was unrelentingly male. Exceedingly handsome. Even unconscious, he exuded a sense of leashed power, like a sleeping cougar.

And she had to get him out of the car before he drowned.

But how? The man looked to be a muscular six-footer; she was a very pregnant five-three. She couldn't even get her hand far enough inside the car to touch him.

Dani tugged on her lower lip for a second.

Then, taking a deep breath, she did the only thing she could think of. She started shouting.

Regret was still there as a thought slowly emerged from the blackness. *So this...is...being dead.*

Josh struggled to form another thought, but— What *was* that infernal noise?

"Darn it, wake up! Come on, mister. Open your eyes!"

With a groan, he obeyed. *Where*— Was he in a car? The windshield looked like a silvery net—except for a hole on the right side.

Through the opening, he could see a light. He'd heard about that. He was supposed to go toward it, wasn't he?

A face appeared, floating in the light. A beautiful face. Soft glowing skin, a wide luscious mouth, huge greenish eyes. Surrounded by a fuzzy, burnished halo. *An angel. Straight out of della Robbia.*

"That's it. Wake up."

Josh blinked. One or two angels. He couldn't tell for sure. Their edges blurred and melded as they gestured frantically. He closed his eyes. *Better.*

"Are you hurt?"

Sensation crept to the front of his awareness. He was cold. Wet. And…everything hurt. Especially his head.

"Answer me!" She sounded scared.

Huh? Angels weren't afraid, were they?

"C-can you move?" This one was. Palpably.

Through the reverberating pain, Josh knew he ought to ease the angel's anxiety. "Yes, ma'am…." He flapped a hand to demonstrate his mobility.

"Come on, then! There's no time to waste. Crawl out through the windshield."

No. His head would explode if he moved. *Better just stay here….* "Don't want to," Josh mumbled.

"I didn't ask you if you want to, mister. I told you to move. Now do it!"

Bossy damned angel, Josh thought grumpily, but began to inch his body up the steering wheel at her insistent nagging, gritting his teeth against the waves of pain that washed over him.

A couple of eternities later, Josh heaved himself over the

dashboard and partially through the windshield opening. It seemed to be lined with blue nylon. A small angelic hand grabbed a wad of shirt and added its upward pressure to his efforts.

Eventually, he lay on rough, wet rock.

His rescuer sat beside him, breathing raggedly.

Breathing. Not an angel, then. Real. Me, too.... Yes, now it seemed obvious. He was still alive.

For one thing, he hurt too much to be dead.

Josh opened his eyes briefly and stared at a shapely nearby ankle. He wondered vaguely who it belonged to. But he couldn't focus right now. On anything, except— "Thanks." He let his eyelids fall shut again, hoping to ease the dizziness.

"Don't thank me yet." The words were tinged with a soft Southern accent—and more concern.

"Why not?" Josh countered, although he barely managed to form the words through the whirling in his head. "You got me out of the car. You saved my life."

"Not yet."

"Close enough." Keeping his eyes shut, Josh pressed his cheek contentedly against the stone. A little rain didn't bother him. He'd just take a short nap and...

A faint whiff of flowers and woman alerted him to her closeness. Then his rescuer's hands were gentle as they smoothed over his limbs and fingered a lump on his temple.

Her heart, however, was as hard as surgical steel. Her next words proved it. "You're soaked," the woman barked. "And this is the desert—with night comin' on fast. You ever heard of hypothermia, mister? Get up!"

Damn the woman! Okay, he owed her his life, but—

Josh pulled himself to his knees. And threw up. "Sorry," he croaked after his stomach stopped cartwheeling.

"Don't worry about it," she said, amusement now warming her tone. "I've sure done my share of that."

Josh didn't get the joke. It didn't matter; a second later,

Ms. Stormtrooper dragged him to his feet. Made him slosh a hundred miles or so through a snarling stream. Forced him to stagger uphill for a couple of centuries....

He threw up again. Conquered a tall step. Crossed a creaking floor. Wondered why heaven smelled like corn bread, then remembered he was still in Texas.

The gentle hands touched him again and his clothes went away....

Then he was warm and dry and lying on something soft. In the distance he heard his rescuer tell him not to go to sleep. Every time he opened his eyes, though, the room started spinning. Darkness like thick, black cotton pressed in around him.

But he was alive. He'd been given a second chance. Josh felt a smile curve his mouth. Okay, he'd admit it. His life *had* seemed empty lately. But that could change. *Would* change. Because now he had time to fill the emptiness.

"Thanks," he whispered. "Thanks again."

With a slow sigh, Josh let the blackness claim him....

Chapter Two

Dani's elbow slipped off the armrest—her eyes flew open. Darn, she'd drifted off again. Sunlight streamed through the window over the sink. *Oh, no...* It had still been dark outside the last time she'd checked on her unexpected guest.

With a soft grunt, Dani maneuvered herself out of the battered armchair, then quietly crossed the narrow cabin floor to look at the man in her bed.

That ribbon of heat coiled through her again.

It was ridiculous, but with the heavy beard shadowing his hard jaw, he was even more attractive this morning than he'd been last night. *When I undressed him.*

The heat got hotter; the ribbon coiled tighter.

She could still feel his sleek, hard muscles and the smooth, taut skin she'd encountered when she'd peeled off his wet clothes. Still see the broad expanse of his shoulders, his flat stomach, his narrow hips. Her fingertips still tingled from the crisp hair on his chest and legs and around—

Dani stopped the tantalizing recital with a wry grimace. She'd undressed Jimmy plenty of times after he'd started coming in drunk every night, she reminded herself. It was no big deal.

Well, actually, this man's was....

Oh, just make sure he's not in a coma, Dani told herself, and carefully lifted one eyelid, then the other. With a sigh of relief, she noted that the pupils, unequal when she'd begun checking last night, were now the same size and reacted to the morning light.

Gently, Dani let the second lid drop. It hardly seemed fair. This man with the magnificent body and boldly masculine features—and a car that, even wrecked, was worth more than her truck running—this man also had the most beautiful eyes she'd ever seen. They were a rich, vibrant turquoise—the color of the Caribbean sea on travel posters.

Jimmy's eyes had been brown. Just brown. Like his hair. And he'd never had a chance to outgrow the gangly adolescent stage; his low-life friends had seen to that.

Dani allowed herself one short sigh for what-might-have-been. Even though her romantic illusions had been crushed by reality long before Jimmy died, she would have made a satisfactory life out of raising her children and providing her husband with a warm, welcoming home. If she'd had the chance.

But Jimmy had chosen booze and self-pity instead of her. And all her love, concern and caring hadn't helped him grow up. *Or kept him home.*

And it still hurt....

Well, at least she knew better than to ever get involved again. Romance was just a liability now, a distraction she couldn't afford.

Still... Yielding to temptation, Dani smoothed back a strand of thick, honey-gold hair. The heartbreaker in her bed simply oozed raw male power and sensuality—even while he was asleep! He must have women throwing themselves at him from all directions.

And how many have you caught, Mr. Joshua Michael

Walker? Dani recalled the Virginia driver's license she'd found in his wallet when she'd looked for an information card listing next of kin—just in case.

Michael... She'd been considering that name for a boy. Emily, if it was a girl.... *Plenty of time to decide once it's here,* she told herself, absently massaging a dull ache low in her back as she turned and headed for the cabin's tiny bathroom. She'd get cleaned up and start breakfast, she decided, before waking her guest.

As usual, the lack of hot water speeded Dani through her morning routine, but as she changed into clean clothes and tugged the shirt over her rounded abdomen, she frowned. The baby was awfully quiet this morning.

At least her backache was gone. Maybe the rest of her problems would disappear that easily, too.

After quietly liberating a saucepan from the small stack of dishes on the drainboard, she measured water into it and set it on the stove. Then, while the water heated, she tried to figure out how to send her visitor on his way before he asked any awkward questions.

Dani smoothed her hand over her precious cargo, but inspiration still didn't come. *The Queen of Coping's drawing a blank today.*

The lid on the saucepan started to jitter. Grateful for the distraction, Dani shook oats into the boiling water and began stirring. With her other hand, she rubbed the ache that had returned to her lower back.

By the time the oatmeal was ready for the last of her brown sugar and raisins, the pain had faded again. But the baby still hadn't kicked. Dani bit her lip as she added the flavorings to the hot cereal. If something was wrong... If anything happened to her baby...

Dani stirred harder, trying to dissolve the fear suddenly choking her.

Even before the soft sounds and oddly familiar smell opened his eyes, Josh remembered...*everything.* The flash flood. Being banged around like the tennis ball in a championship match. The angel who'd ordered him out of his sinking car. Being cold and wet, then warm and dry.

He'd been lucky, that was for damned sure. But... *Now what?*

One part of him wanted to forget the whole near-death experience and just slide back into his old routine.

But another part insisted he remember what he'd discovered: something *was* missing from his life. *Okay, but—* Josh grimaced at the rough ceiling overhead.

But nothing, he told himself. *Only fools waste second chances. And any fool could tell you how to fill that emptiness inside.*

"Hell," he whispered to the lumber overhead. He still wanted a baby, but the biology hadn't changed in the past six years: fatherhood still required a woman's participation. And after Carrie, he could never trust a woman enough to share such an intimate bond.

Which meant no babies for Josh Walker.

Well, there were other meaningful things in life.

Find someone...help them. His sister-in-law's advice floated through his brain again. Okay, when he got home, he'd see about signing up to tutor poor kids or something.

"Oh, good. You're awake."

His lips quirking at the unintentional irony, Josh glanced up. And rational thought disappeared, buried in an explosive, visceral male reaction he'd never before experienced.

Yesterday's angel stood over him, her soft, full lips curved in a sweet smile that made him long to trace her mouth with his finger, then with his own lips, then plunder the moist, warm depths with his tongue....

Shocked by the intensity of his desire, Josh blinked, then blinked again as her thick braid slid forward over her shoulder to dangle an inch from his nose. The rope of hair glowed like polished maple; his hand itched to take its silky weight.

"How do you feel?" she asked, her green eyes clouded with concern.

Very alive. Very male. Very ready to prove it.

Trying to slow his pounding pulse, Josh took a deep breath and caught her scent: sweetness and soap and... *woman*. It made him ache, then turn on his side to hide his body's instant response.

"Fine, Ms.— I'm sorry I don't know your name," he mumbled, fighting desperately to regain control. This *didn't* happen to him.

But it *was*.

"Dani Caldwell," the woman said, then bit her lip. "Please—forget you heard that."

"Whatever you want, Dani," he agreed. "You saved my life. Words seem pretty inadequate, but—thanks." *I wonder if her skin feels as soft as it looks.* As he propped himself up on one elbow, Josh's free hand moved toward his rescuer.

The woman stepped back. Good. Maybe he could think straight if she wasn't close enough to caress.

Josh tore his gaze from his rescuer's angelic face. Looked downward. "You're pregnant!"

"I believe you're right." Her grin invited him to share her joy.

Like hell. "What in damnation were you thinking of, lady?" he demanded, sitting up and wadding the blanket with clenched fists to keep from shaking the little idiot. "You could have harmed your baby! Where the hell's your husband? What kind of knucklehead lets his wife risk his unborn child by charging headlong into raging floodwaters? He ought to—"

"He can't," Dani interrupted. "He's dead."

Josh stared at her, shocked speechless. He'd spent years grieving beneath his icy outer layer because—thanks to Carrie's betrayal—he would never hold his baby. This woman carried a child who would never know its father's protective embrace. "Oh, God, Dani," he whispered. "I'm sorry. So sorry."

She stood looking at him for a moment, her eyes dark and distant, one hand slowly rubbing her back. "Well, 'sorry' never changed facts," she said at last, "but...thanks.

"They should be dry now, so here. Get dressed." Scooping up a pile of clothes draped over the foot of the bed, she dumped them on his lap. Which was a tad sensitive—since he was still more than a tad aroused.

Josh grabbed the clothes in self-defense. "Th-thank you."

As he sorted through the apparel, Dani turned toward the stove. Her braid hung almost to her waist, he noticed. Then had to clamp a lid on heated images of her above him with it loose, streaming over her breasts, brushing his— *She's a grieving widow,* Josh reminded himself as he shoved his legs into stiff jeans. *Carrying proof of her love.*

"Breakfast is ready. I hope you like oatmeal."

She didn't *act* grief-stricken, but she had a right to handle her sorrow her own way. Josh knew from his own bitter experience that talking never changed anything, anyway. And he was starving, but— "Oatmeal? I'd rather have eggs and bacon. Biscuits and honey."

"Me, too." At Dani's low laugh, Josh's thoughts of food were replaced by another sort of hunger.

Facts were the best weapon against dangerous feelings. He knew *that* from experience, too. "How old are you?" he blurted, desperate to control his inappropriate response to this woman.

"Twenty-three," she answered, spreading her fingers over her beach ball stomach and frowning.

She looked younger. Made him feel ancient. "How long ago did your—"

"Six months. Now, about breakfast, Mr. Walker..."

"Call me Josh." He wanted his name on those lush lips. Instead of painful memories. "But how did you—"

"I looked in your wallet." She turned so quickly, her braid went flying. "Everything's still there."

"I'm sure it is," he agreed as he climbed out of bed, buttoned his fly—with difficulty—then pulled on his shirt.

Hell, for saving his life, she could have every gold, platinum or purple card she found, all the cash, whatever. He told her so.

"I didn't save your life, Josh! I—" She gestured impatiently. "I broke your windshield. Please—just eat your breakfast and go."

Fat chance. Josh Walker always paid his debts and he owed Dani Caldwell. But he reserved arguing for the courtroom. "Okay," he said mildly.

As he headed toward the table, Dani retreated. As if... "You're not afraid of me, are you?" Josh asked. "I swear— I'd never hurt a woman!"

Dani's eyes looked into a distance he couldn't see. "I'm sure you mean that," she said, "but...well, intentions make good paving material." Her voice was too old, too resigned for someone so young. Someone with a baby coming and *no father for it.*

"You can trust me, Dani." Josh's low voice stroked over her skin like rich, dark velvet. He seemed to fill the room with his large, lean frame, with his hard masculinity. "Are you in trouble? Let me help you."

Dani fought an urge to accept his offer. "I don't need any help," she insisted, mostly to remind herself. *Didn't marriage teach me anything? Leaning on someone just means you fall over when they leave.*

Josh did something with his jaw that brought granite to mind. "Then I'll get out of your way," he said stiffly. "May I use your phone to call a tow truck?"

"Sorry." She shook her head. "No telephone."

"Can you give me a lift to town, then?" Icicles dripped from every word.

"No wheels, either," Dani confessed, flashing a rueful smile.

"You mean, you're stranded out here? In your condition?" Josh looked as if he didn't know whether to sit there stupefied or jump up, furious. "Are you crazy, woman?"

"Just a little unlucky, that's all." Dani willed herself to believe it. But that darned backache kept coming back and the baby still hadn't moved. What if something was seriously wrong?

"Un*lucky?*" Josh croaked, those beautiful eyes wide with disbelief.

He was still sputtering when heavy knuckles made contact with the door. Dani seized the interruption. "Who's there?" she called.

"County sheriff," came the answer in a deep West Texas twang.

Terror-stricken, Dani turned to Josh. "Please," she whispered. "Please. Tell the sheriff I'm with you. Tell him—anything. Except my name."

For one long moment, Josh gazed at her, his eyes narrow slivers of glacial ice. Then a corner of his mouth quirked and he shook his head derisively. "I never did learn to ask the right questions at the right time," he said softly.

Dani closed her eyes to gather her strength. She was going to need it. The visitor knocked again.

"Just a minute!" Josh shouted, then lowered his voice. "I owe you my life, Dani," he said, "but I'm an attorney. Aiding a felon is grounds for disbarment."

"I haven't committed any crime," she snapped, rubbing her back.

"Then tell me why you're hiding."

Dani chewed her lip but she had no choice. She knew whose side the sheriff would take if he discovered her identity. This stranger was her only chance; she had to trust him. Simple but scary. She hadn't trusted anyone since...*Jimmy, who'd proven himself untrustworthy in the end.*

Taking a deep breath, Dani said, "My husband was killed by a stray bullet when a fight broke out at the bar that had become his second home. His parents blamed me for his lack of ambition, his choice of friends, and his death. And now they want custody of their grandchild. I've refused, of course, but they're wealthy and have contacts all over the state. Obviously I can't even hold a job right now...."

Josh suddenly towered over her, his hands on his hips. "Sounds as if they can offer the child more than you can."

"I'm not giving up my baby," Dani retorted, balling her hands into fists. "I don't care what *things* they can give it, this baby is mine!"

Those turquoise eyes flared into blue fire, then Josh touched her cheek gently with one fingertip. She could feel it all the way to her toes, even through the backache gripping her now like a bulldog on a bone.

"Okay, sweetheart, okay." Josh jerked his hand away. "I guess I can perjure myself this once." He crossed the cabin in one stride.

Pulling open the door, Josh leaned a broad shoulder against the door frame and greeted the beefy, leather-skinned man standing on the porch. "Morning, Sheriff."

"B'lieve it is," the man drawled, hooking his thumbs in the service belt of his khaki uniform. He looked sleepy and slow, but Dani doubted it. Law enforcement in rural counties only meant dealing with fewer people, not less complex ones.

"Name's Lopez," the sheriff announced, removing his wire-rimmed sunglasses and hanging them by one earpiece from his starched shirt pocket. "And you are?"

"Josh Walker...and wife."

After a brief, searching look, Lopez said, "Quite a storm last night. Been out since dawn, checking on damage. That your car down in the creek?"

"Yes. My wife and I barely got out in time. We took

refuge here last night.'' Josh did his granite-jaw exhibition again. ''Hope that isn't a problem, Officer.''

The sheriff shrugged. ''Real problem's gonna be gettin' yore vee-hicle outta that arroyo,'' he drawled. ''Don't know if Vern can get his tow truck close enough to—''

Dani didn't hear the rest. A fresh fist of pain hit her, then—a gush of warm wetness between her legs. Her knees threatened to go on strike and she blindly clutched at Josh for support.

His arm instantly wrapped around her. ''Wh-what is it, Dani? What happened?''

Before she could answer, Lopez chuckled. ''As the father of five, I'd say the lady's water broke.'' Pushing the brim of his Stetson up with his thumb, he addressed Dani. ''You havin' pains yet, ma'am?''

She managed to nod. ''I—I guess I've been having them since I woke up this morning, b-but...'' She bit her lip.

''But what?'' Josh demanded.

His arm still crushed her against his side. Dani didn't resist; she needed his strength right now. She wanted this baby so much, but— ''Th-the pains aren't right!''

The sheriff whipped his sunglasses out of his pocket, snapped them open with a flick of his wrist and slid them on his face, his sleepy demeanor instantly replaced by cool efficiency. ''They got a clinic in No Lake. I'll hustle on down to the car and radio the doc. You bring yore wife.''

As the sheriff spun on his heel and disappeared down the trail, Josh turned to Dani. ''What do you mean, not right?'' he demanded, his hands wrapped around her upper arms, his azure eyes hot and intense.

''They're in my back, not here.'' Dani's hand covered her abdomen.

Josh's grip eased. ''My sister-in-law had back labor,'' he said. ''Twice. And both babies were perfect.''

This is normal. Relief dissolved the fear washing through

her, and without thinking, Dani aimed a thank-you kiss at Josh's cheek.

As her lips neared the beard-roughened surface, she caught a faint whiff of pine and a unique male scent she instinctively recognized as his. Then Josh turned his head and mouth met mouth—one warm and soft, one cool and firm. A momentary hesitation...then someone deepened the kiss. Stars exploded. Volcanoes blew apart. The earth shifted on its axis—and babies and back pains were forgotten for one eternal second while heat and passion consumed her. Someone moaned, the sound deep and throaty. Dani thrust her fingers into Josh's thick, silky hair. He wrapped her braid around his wrist—

Reality finally intruded. *I'm having a baby. Jimmy's baby.* "I—I'm sorry," she whispered as she pulled back. "I just... Thank you for telling me about your sister-in-law."

"Any time, lady." Josh gave a ragged laugh as he raked shaking fingers through his hair and let out a deep breath. "Except now, that is. We've got places to go."

His briskness told Dani that the errant kiss hadn't affected him. A tendril of pain helped her ignore the desire still racing through her veins. "I n-need to get the b-baby's things," she said.

Josh growled. "Where?"

She pointed to a yellow quilted bag; he snatched it up. Then the darned man scooped her up, too. He carried her out of the cabin and down the path with long, swift strides, placing her in the sheriff's car as if she were fine Austrian crystal.

He balked, however, when the sheriff ordered him into the back seat, too. "Look, I'm not— Just take her to the doctor, okay? I'll, er, wait here."

"You're the reason she's in this condition, son," the sheriff snapped. "Seems to me, you oughta finish what you start."

Josh scowled. Dani wasn't his woman; her "condition"

wasn't his fault. And Carrie had never given him the chance to finish what he'd accidentally started.

Dani groaned.

Instantly, Josh was beside her in the car. "Another pain?"

She nodded, her face pinched and tight, those sensual lips pressed into a thin line.

Which left nothing to do but— "Shh," he murmured, pulling her onto his lap. "I'm here, Dani. I won't leave you." He wrapped his arms around her, held her tightly against his chest. *It feels right.* As right as that spine-tingling kiss a minute ago.

All of which was completely wrong. Dammit, he didn't respond like this to a woman, *any* woman—especially one having another man's baby!

"Thank you for not giving me away," Dani whispered as the sheriff eased the patrol car onto the road. "I owe you."

Josh just snorted at that nonsense. Of their own accord, his arms tightened around her.

"I don't mean to tell you your business, Lopez," he snarled, "but floor it, will you? The woman's having a baby!"

"I ain't licensed to fly, son. We'll get there. Don't worry." The damned fool slowed down then, just to go through a blind curve.

At last, they reached a town. The sheriff spun the steering wheel, then stood on the brakes and screeched to a halt in front of a metal prefab building.

"Here y'are," he announced. "No Lake Medical Clinic. Told ya we'd get here in time."

"Thanks, Sheriff." Josh jerked open the car door. "I, uh, I—"

Even Lopez's laugh had a Texas twang. "'Pology accepted, son. Best get yore wife inside now. The doc'll take it from here. And good luck to ya."

Josh kept his hands steady and gentle as he eased Dani

out of the car, and carried her carefully up the clinic steps.

The place was deserted—except for one small, mahogany-skinned, too-damned-young man wearing a white knit shirt, nylon shorts and striped kneesocks. "Good Sunday morning to you," he said as he directed Josh to an examining room and helped him settle Dani on the table there. "I am Dr. Ravjani, playing soccer only moments ago."

"Josh Walker. This is Dani." Josh watched her anxiously. Her eyes were closed again as she rode out another contraction, breathing deeply.

"Very happy to be meeting you." Ravjani grinned as he began taking Dani's blood pressure. "I am guessing first baby. Right?"

"Yes," she exhorted. "But my due date isn't for two more weeks."

"Oh, first babies are notorious for not heeding the calendar," the doctor said cheerfully.

When Dani offered a tentative smile in response, Josh turned to leave.

"Good idea!" Ravjani crowed, grabbing Josh's arm. "I will help Mrs. Dani into a sterile gown while you are washing up to your elbows." For a small man, Ravjani had a tenacious grip. Josh found himself being hustled from the room and down a hallway. "Then I will examine your wife while you are comforting her."

Josh shook his head. Tried to free his arm. The little man's grip tightened.

"This was not a question, Josh Walker. My nurse is barbecuing her boyfriend today, so I am needing your help." The doctor shoved him into a tiny bathroom. "Mrs. Dani is already afraid of what she isn't knowing. Now I am an excellent doctor, you understand, but my English—I may not be saying the comforting clichés correctly to keep her focus off the pain. I tell you—thinking about it will only make this delivery harder." The little man shook a finger under

Josh's nose. "For the baby's sake, you must be helping me."

With that, Ravjani disappeared.

Well, hell. Josh reached for the soap. He'd spent six years mourning his lost baby. As he scrubbed his hands and forearms nearly raw, some scorekeeper in his head observed, *Helping Dani deliver her baby will give you part of what Carrie denied you.*

Besides, he owed Dani Caldwell his life. And even if he didn't, no man worth the name turned away from a woman in need.

Josh grabbed a wad of paper towels and dried his hands as he hurried back to the examining room.

Dani gave him a smile, but— Yes, some fear lurked in those luminous green eyes. So Josh wrapped his fingers around hers. Squeezed gently. Tried to act reassuring. Probably failed. Complications worthy of a soap opera kept flashing through his head.

After Ravjani examined Dani—while Josh examined his impressive medical credentials on the wall—he assured them everything was proceeding normally. "Rest between contractions," he advised, patting Dani's hand. "This will be taking some time. Do not become anxious," he added, spearing Josh with a significant look. Then he wandered off to catch up on paperwork.

A tear slid down Dani's cheek and lingered on the edge of her full lower lip. He remembered how soft her mouth felt under his, how sweet she tasted....

"Dammit. Please, Dani—don't cry!"

Thank heavens. A distraction. Through her own anxiety, Dani recognized the discomfort beneath Josh's gruffness. She knew men weren't very good with the messy parts of life; Jimmy had especially hated her tears.

And what good were they, after all? They didn't change reality.

"You don't need to stay," she said, feigning nonchalance. "My husband would have been long gone by now."

"No man would miss his kid's birth," Josh declared in a voice like hammered steel.

"Do you and your wife—" She gasped as a contraction hit.

"I'm not married."

Did he think biting off the words could hide the raw anguish and grief echoing through them? Despite herself, Dani wondered at their cause.

"Quit wasting your energy," he commanded. "I'm not leaving you."

His deep, quiet voice offered support, like a strong pair of hands. Okay, she'd admit it: she didn't want to face this alone. But did she dare accept this stranger's help?

As the contraction eased, Dani gazed up into Josh's beautiful azure eyes. She saw apprehension in their depths, but determination was there, too. This was a man, not a boy. He carried scars—that still hurt, apparently—but maybe they'd made him strong. The way disappointment had weaned her from dreams and toughened her.

Another wave of pain pulled at her. "Then make yourself useful," she gasped. "Talk. About anything. Just—talk."

And so, through long, draining hours and slowly escalating waves of pain, she clung to Josh's strong, hard hand and his deep, smooth voice as he talked of his boyhood in Montana and asked about life in Lufkin.

Late in the afternoon, the contractions changed. Dani groaned, fighting the urge to push.

Josh leaped to his feet. "I'll get Ravjani!"

"No need," the doctor proclaimed as he bustled into the room to stand between Dani's legs. "Ravjani is here and, ah, just in time."

His bubbly confidence was reassuring, Dani thought hazily, even if his English was slightly fractured.

"Look, Mr. Walker," Dr. Ravjani ordered. "Your child is arriving."

As Dani lay panting for the few seconds she sensed were all she'd have, she watched Josh reluctantly peek over the doctor's shoulder.

Beneath his tan, Josh's color faded; his expression wavered between dismay and disgust. Alarmed, Dani cried, "Josh! What's wrong?"

"Your baby is crowning, that's all," said Ravjani. He smirked at Dani. "Perhaps your husband is one of those large, macho men who faints at the sight of one of nature's miracles."

The greenish undertones to Josh's skin turned greener. "I... It's too— You can't— Do something, dammit!" Had Carrie known about this...this whole appalling birth process? Was that why—

Dr. Ravjani chuckled. "I am not the one who must be doing now. Your wife must begin pushing your creation out of his comfortable home. And you are still the cheerleader, Mr. Walker."

Begin pushing? What the hell did the idiot think she'd been doing? For hours and hours already. And there was *more?*

"Mr. Walker. If I ask for the tray, I am meaning that," Ravjani barked, pointing to a shallow metal dish filled with gleaming surgical instruments. "And I am needing it quickly."

The floor tilted. Blackness crowded the edges of Josh's vision.

Then, like yesterday, Dani's voice, somehow urgent and calm at the same time, cut through the darkness. "Josh. I'll be fine. Women have been having babies for thousands of years. Just come hold my hand."

Like yesterday, he obeyed that voice. Then following Ravjani's instructions, Josh moved around to the head of the exam table so he could brace Dani's back with his chest.

As he touched her, moved her braid to the side, clasped her hands, the black mist cleared. Once again, Dani had rescued him—this time from embarrassing himself.

"Push when you are ready," the doctor told Dani.

"Aauunnh!" She bowed forward, rigid with effort.

Nothing happened. Eventually, she went limp.

"Again."

She made another magnificent, shaking effort—her chin on her chest, her teeth gritted.

Still nothing happened, except Ravjani in that damned calm voice said, "Once more."

Dani shook and pushed, her face white with the strain.

"Another time, please."

"Uuhn—nah!"

"It's a boy," Ravjani announced happily as he lifted a red and white streaked...*thing* and laid it on Dani's stomach. It scrunched up its wrinkled face and gave a little cry of protest.

"Oh, isn't he beautiful?" Dani breathed. Beneath her fatigue radiated wonder and joy and exultation.

Disappointment closed Josh's throat. All that agony, all that valiant effort—and this was the result? He'd never seen an uglier being. "Oh, Dani, I'm so sorry."

Ravjani whisked the thing away. Josh cradled Dani's head against his chest. Tried to think of something comforting to say. Got distracted by her satiny skin and the damp, silky curls that coiled around her face and over his fingers.

"There. All presentable." Ravjani dumped a neatly wrapped bundle in his arms. "Mr. Walker, say hello to your son."

Hesitantly, Josh looked down at the newborn infant in his arms. "Oh, Dani, you're right," he breathed, barely able to form the words. Well, he was busy—falling hopelessly, ecstatically, deliriously in love. "He *is* beautiful." And talented. Just lying there, this tiny baby filled a man's empty heart. Amazing.

No, a miracle. "Thank you." Overwhelmed by the emotions coursing through him, Josh wanted to ravage Dani's lush mouth. He settled for a light kiss on her forehead. "Oh, Dani—thank you."

"Show your gratitude by doing housework," the doctor suggested, plucking the precious bundle from Josh's arms, which immediately missed the weight. "Now, little one, meet your mother." Ravjani handed the baby to Dani.

Who smiled radiantly at...*her son.*

Mine, too!

Well, not technically, legally or biologically, but... Determination as implacable as forge-tempered steel formed within him. After years of icy grief and anger and anguish, by a freak twist of fate, Josh had a baby—and he wasn't giving it up. Not yet, anyway. *Only a fool wastes second chances.*

Which brought him back to Carrie and the baby she'd denied him. Dammit, why hadn't she—

...*Stop picking at the scab.*

Right. He had more important things to think about than the past. Like the rest of his life. The baby he'd just seen born.

And the woman who'd given him both.

When Ravjani told him to go away while "we do a little mending," Josh went. As far as the waiting room. There, he slumped in a molded plastic chair and tried to formulate an agenda.

High on the list: concretely expressing his gratitude to Dani Caldwell. For saving his life. And giving him the most incredible, fulfilling experience of his life.

Most urgent item, though? Figure out how to get his hands on that baby again.

What are my chances of persuading Dani to let me take the baby home to Virginia? he wondered.

Of course, the baby's mother would have to come, too....

For a moment he felt Dani's warm, soft mouth under his again and wondered if he was playing with fire.

No, he wouldn't be stupid enough to kiss her again. He knew better than most how to avoid getting burned.

Anyway, how tempting were a few bone-melting, earth-shattering kisses when he could hold that baby in his arms?

Sometime later, Ravjani handed Josh a list of things Dani and the baby would need, could do and should avoid. "If you wish to be a good father," he said sternly, "you will see that these instructions are followed by the letter."

After scanning it quickly, Josh flashed the doctor a blinding smile and thanked him for the ammunition.

Chapter Three

Dani twisted the motel showerhead and stepped under the spray. Leaning against the wall, she let the warm water sluice over her. "This is ridiculous," she murmured.

She'd had the baby three whole days ago. How could she still be so exhausted?

And what would she have done without Josh Walker? she wondered. Without his reassurance about back labor being normal, without his deep voice encouraging her and his hard chest supporting her, lending her strength while she pushed and pushed against the wall of pain....

And afterward... *I was about as energetic as a hibernating turtle.*

Dani turned so the water could cascade over her hair.

Josh, on the other hand, had come striding back into the room and told her not to chew her lip off. Then he'd practically ordered the doctor to bring them here, contacted the town druggist and demanded that he not only open his store—on a Sunday evening—but personally deliver the items on the list Dr. Ravjani had given him. Arriving at the town's only motel, he'd continued to issue commands like the crew chief in a disaster drill. A crib for the baby. Extra pillows. Meals and diapers—even a nightgown for her.

True, it was old-fashioned, macho bullying at its worst, but at the time, it was just what she needed.

When she'd tried to protest that she didn't want to be a bother, Josh had muttered something about just playing his husband role, keeping the story straight until they left No Lake.

Dani blinked back some stupid tears. Jimmy had been the perfect prom date, a great boyfriend with whom to exchange senior rings and notes in class. But a thoughtful, dependable, supportive husband? Dani shook her head sadly.

Josh Walker, on the other hand, could give lessons! That first day, he'd helped her in and out of bed as if she was made of fine bone china. He'd brought meals to her from the café across the street. Yesterday, he'd borrowed Ravjani's car and collected her belongings from the cabin.

He'd even helped with the baby. *Which Jimmy hadn't even wanted....*

Those dumb tears threatened again, so she thought about the first time Josh had insisted on changing a diaper—his big strong hands had ripped the tape strip right off. The next attempt had fallen to the floor when Josh proudly lifted the baby to display his handiwork.

Jimmy would have stalked away then—unable to deal with failure long enough to succeed. Josh had simply flashed a wry smile, made some comment about "third time lucky" and reached for another diaper. Moments later, with a triumphant flourish, he'd handed her the securely diapered baby.

Dani sighed. Every baby should have a father, whether he did any diapering or not. Hers would only have... *A mother who loves him with all her heart. A mom he can always depend on.*

"That's not so bad, is it, Michael?" she whispered into the falling water.

Michael James Caldwell. A good, strong name for a boy—and for the man he'd grow into. If she did her job.

The tears escaped and poured down her face. "Oh, stop it," she told herself, grabbing the little bar of soap. She rubbed it over the washcloth, then doggedly spread lather over her body. "Cope, don't mope—remember?"

Her goals for the immediate future were simple: get back her energy, care for Michael, find a job.

And repay Josh Walker. While she washed and rinsed her hair, Dani calculated that, intangibles aside, her debt to the man in the next room already exceeded her meager savings.

Still simple, if not exactly easy.

Not easy at all. After drying off and getting dressed, Dani felt as limp as unset gelatin, but managed to braid her reddish-brown mop, then checked on her sleeping son—and couldn't help touching him in wonder. I really ought to straighten the room before lunch arrives, she thought, smiling at Michael's cloud of pale, fine hair.

Oh, be honest—it's Josh you'd like to impress, not a hamburger.

It was almost noon, which meant he'd soon be bringing lunch. And if Michael was awake, she'd get her meal with a gruff order to eat while he took care of the baby.

Seeing her tiny son cradled against one of Josh's massive shoulders made her insides heat.

The kiss they'd shared seared through her again and she wished...

Crossing to the bed, Dani jerked the covers into place, then dumped the baby's things on the bed and started reorganizing them. She would not waste her time on impossible dreams.

They weren't very big dreams—a home, a family, she told herself for the eight millionth time. Why had Jimmy run from them? *And me?*

Slowly, Dani collapsed on the bed, still clutching the little snap-front shirt she'd just folded. She knew there was no answer; she was just tired. *And they were my dreams,* she thought sleepily, *not his.* Against her will, Dani's eyes drifted closed....

Shutting the door with his hip, Josh tossed the package of diapers at a chair and dropped the food sack on the dresser. Then he shoved yesterday's shirt aside and plopped down on the bed. After adjusting the pillows behind his head, he picked up the remote, crossed his ankles and tried to get interested in the heated discussion on television. Couldn't. He really didn't give a damn about spouses who dated their ex-spouse's ex-spouse or whatever today's theme was.

He wanted to be with his baby, who was right next door.

Leaning sideways, Josh moved aside a balled-up sock so he could see the bedside clock.

Good. Nearly noon. In a few minutes he'd stroll over to the connecting door, knock and poke his head into Dani's room. While he asked if she was hungry yet, he'd get a glimpse of Michael.

Josh grinned at the couple crying on TV. If he was really lucky, Dani would be in the bathroom or sleeping or something and he'd get to tiptoe over to the crib. Have a few minutes to absorb more fascinating details about that darling baby. Maybe even reach down and stroke his unbelievably soft skin.

The talk show host hit a sympathetic pose for the camera. Josh curled his fingers into fists. Dammit—he needed that baby!

Sunday, while the motel manager had hunted up a crib and the doc put Dani to bed, he'd gotten almost twenty uninterrupted minutes to hold Michael. To marvel at his incredible, tiny fingers and toes.

Since then, however, the situation had deteriorated severely. Yesterday, Dani had said something about not needing to hover over them.

Hover? He'd barely been near the baby! Or her. He'd only been allowed to burp the little guy a couple of times. So far, he'd only managed to change eight or nine diapers. Just one little shirt. One!

Josh pulled off his boots and let them drop. The couple on TV turned to shout at the audience.

He needed more time with Michael.

The talk show couple embraced. The studio audience applauded. Josh scowled and began surfing through the channels. He had to convince Dani to let him take her husband's baby to Virginia.

But how?

Persuasive argument? Bribery? *Seduction?*

Josh paused at a tennis match, but one of the players was positioned behind a T-shirt draped over the corner of the TV set.

Too damned dangerous. With her luminous jade-green eyes, incredible coppery hair and smooth, creamy skin, Dani Caldwell roused protective, possessive instincts in a man. And that made him vulnerable.

Josh mashed the remote once more. He refused to let another woman hurt him.

Through the sizzle of mushrooms in a sauté pan and some sappy theme music, Josh heard the softest of whimpers.

Instantly he was on his feet, flying through the connecting doorway.

The scene that met his eyes was...his worst nightmare.

Michael lay on his back in the crib, kicking his adorable little legs. Dani was sitting on her bed, short tendrils of hair writhing gloriously around her flushed cheeks, her emerald eyes glowing beneath heavy lids.

Desire streaked through him like hot lightning.

Gritting his teeth against it, Josh concentrated on the disaster: she was packing Michael's things into that damned yellow quilted bag.

"What the hell do you think you're doing?" he demanded, then forced his voice to steady. "Sorry. I meant something more like 'Are you sure you should be up? The doctor said you needed plenty of rest.'"

"I've *been* resting." A wry smile quirked those luscious lips into a soft curve as she brushed at her hair with one hand.

Josh's gaze went straight to her full breasts. He should have thought about mother's milk and Michael. Instead, another jolt of pure male desire spiked through him. He wanted his own mouth nuzzling that sweet feminine flesh—

"Josh?" She was looking at him expectantly.

"You, ah, must be feeling stronger, right?"

Dani winced. Pretty blatant hint, she thought, but who can blame him? Why would he want to stick around playing nursemaid to a hick from Lufkin?

"Y-yes." She made herself look straight into his turquoise eyes. It was safer than ogling the rest of him. And that's what she wanted to do because—well, honestly, Josh Walker had looked sexy in wet jeans, and like a Greek statue undressed, but *this*... This ought to be illegal!

The white dress shirt set off his tan the way black velvet sets off priceless diamonds. He'd folded back the sleeves, too, which just emphasized his tanned, muscular forearms. And that hint of dark, crinkly hair at the open neck— Dani knew how it swirled across the broad muscular plane of his chest, then narrowed to a wedge angling downward to... *Control yourself.*

To expensive dark dress slacks and patterned dress socks.

Dani sighed. The man positively radiated sleek virility and mature sophistication. Of course, he wanted her out of his hair.

Well, she had no money, no transportation and no idea where to go, but she still had her pride. "I—I can be packed in twenty minutes." And her manners. "I sure thank you, Josh, for everything you've done for me and Michael. If you'll give me your address, I'll send you the money I owe—''

"No!" Josh barked, thrusting his long, elegant fingers into his thick, golden hair. After a moment he lowered his hand and his voice. "Dammit, Dani, you're in no shape to go anywhere. And you can forget about the money. I want to— Just let me…''

Dani turned away. That deep velvet tone made her want to accept Josh's help, to lean on his strength.

She couldn't allow herself to be tempted. Much as her heart might wish desperately to love again, to trust and share again, Dani couldn't afford the risk. Her heart wasn't hers any longer. It belonged to her son. And Michael needed it whole. "I appreciate your help, Mr. Walker, but I think it's time for us to leave.''

He said a word Dani hoped her son never learned, then Josh's jaw went into granite mode as he spun on his heel and headed for the connecting door. Reaching it, he stopped but didn't turn around. "You should at least have lunch first," he said evenly, as if nothing had upset him.

Dani stared at his rigid back. How could he just cap his feelings like that?

"And by the way," he added just as calmly, "I saw Sheriff Lopez this morning. He wanted to know when *we'd* be heading home.''

"What…'' She had to push the words past frozen tonsils. "What did you tell him?''

Josh turned. "I said—'' Something simmered in his blue orbs, though his tone remained cool. "Well, it doesn't matter now, does it? I should have known you'd never leave Texas.''

With a shrug, he disappeared into his room.

Dani's knees gave way and she sank onto the bed. If the sheriff was asking questions, it was past time to move on. So get going. Make some plans, she told herself, but her mind stayed blank.

She *wouldn't* contact Jimmy's parents. She couldn't give up her son. Not without a fight. And today, she couldn't fight a wet kitten to a draw.

She needed more time!

Josh's last sentence echoed in her head. Could that mean—

Dani stood and twitched her shirt into place. Right now, no possibility was too remote to consider, no action too desperate to contemplate. Of course, he probably didn't mean anything by it, but for Michael's sake, she'd ask.

Maybe she should redo her braid before— "Oh, just get in there and beg before you lose your nerve," she commanded herself. Self agreed, but her feet took a little more convincing. "I'll pay him back," she promised. "Every penny. And I won't cause him any trouble."

One foot moved. The other refused. "And I won't do anything stupid." *Like believe in fairy tales again.*

Her second foot released its deathgrip on the floor.

Checking that Michael was content for the moment, she marched into Josh's room. It looked like the aftermath of a bomb blast, she noted, but refused to let the thought divert her from her mission. Feet slowed, though, as they approached the bed where Josh sprawled. In all his tawny, masculine glory.

I must have been mistaken. But the worst he can say is no. And then I'll— Lifting her chin, Dani addressed the howling coyote print above Josh's head. "What did... You said something about me never leaving Texas?"

Tinny applause erupted from the TV, then Josh touched the remote control and silenced reigned. He crossed his arms over his chest before answering in that same unreadable tone, "Dr. Ravjani said you need at least six weeks of rest. I'm willing to—" His jaw turned to titanium this time. "To see that you get it, but I have a life, too. And it's not in Texas."

Surging hope asked a dumb question. "Wh-where is it?"

She didn't care if it was on the moon, as long as it was far from the Caldwells' influence.

"Fallsboro, Virginia. That's about thirty miles from Washington, D.C."

And plenty of miles from Lufkin. Dani chewed her lip. "And you...you're willing to take me and Michael with you? For six weeks?"

Instead of responding right away, Josh tucked his hands further out of sight under his arms and gazed around the room. "Yes," he said finally. "I was going to offer you...a place to stay until you've gotten your strength back."

"Did... What changed your mind?"

Josh's eyes glowed like faceted aquamarines in full sun as they found her face. "Nothing."

Dani licked suddenly dry lips. He was offering her the one thing she needed: time.

But she wasn't a naive kid any longer who believed in fairy god-hunks and wishes coming true. "Why?"

Which wasn't no. Josh clenched his hands tighter against his sides. If he moved a single muscle, he'd do something explosive to release the tension coiling inside like a mad rattlesnake. He couldn't afford to frighten her. Not now. Not this close.

"Why, Josh?" she repeated.

He looked into the depths of those dark green eyes. *Like shadows in a forest glade.* They offered hope but demanded integrity.

Still, he meant to spin her some tale about paying her back for saving his life. The past was over. And he didn't talk about it, anyway. Not ever.

"Because my child would have been six years old in the fall," he heard himself say. "And...I never got to hold him. Or her. I never even *knew* about him until...it was too late."

"I don't understand."

"Do you think I do?" he shouted, then leaped off the bed and went to stand by the motel window. After a few seconds he remembered to push aside the curtain. Beyond the glass was a parking lot, a highway and about a thousand miles of sage and sand. A landscape as barren as his life.

Dammit, for once he wanted somebody to understand.

But he *needed* Michael.

So he gave Dani facts instead of feelings. "When I was in law school, I...well, my girlfriend accidentally got pregnant."

White-hot anger burned his insides, so he made himself shrug. "It turned out that Carrie's ambitions did not include motherhood. So without consulting me, she had an..." Even now, he couldn't say the word. "She chose not to carry my baby to term," he finished harshly, then waited for Dani's expression of pity. Or revulsion.

Silence filled the room.

Josh turned around. Then blinked. *What the hell?* Dani's green eyes held— Cool disdain?

Dammit, a woman who sacrificed everything to keep her baby should be outraged! He'd laid bare his soul for—indifference?

"I'm sorry, Josh, about...your loss. But—"

A tiny cry came from the next room.

Dani turned immediately to leave. But Josh couldn't wait any longer. He wanted this decided. He needed Michael. And he needed to know now if he could have him.

Luckily, the crying stopped as he moved to block her exit. "Look, Dani, you need help. I—I want what Carrie denied me. Just for a little while. What do you say? Come to Virginia with me."

"We-ell..."

Josh raked his fingers through his hair. Dammit, this was an incredible offer he was making her. She should just take it. He racked his brain for another selling point.

"I have a fully furnished nursery," he said, trying to sound as truthful as possible when uttering such a bald-faced lie. Well, hell. He was under duress, not oath.

"A nursery." A blind man could see the doubt in her eyes.

"Yep, crib and everything. Because, my, ah, brother visits all the time," Josh said. "Brings his kids." And wouldn't that be news to Matt, who hadn't left the ranch in two years! "I'll be at the office all the time...."

She was chewing on that lower lip.

Come on, Walker. You need that baby! "Let me do this for Michael—and for the child I never got to hold..." Josh stuck one hand in his pocket and crossed his fingers. Wished for a rabbit's foot. "Please. Come home with me, Dani."

"H-how soon could we leave?" she asked.

His heart was pounding. *Get it right.* "Tomorrow."

Still gnawing on that lip.

He rushed on. "In the morning. Early."

Her mouth curved slightly. "Okay."

Okay? That meant— Suddenly he was across the room, holding her, bending to take her mouth with his. Wanting—

A furious squalling erupted in the next room. And Dani wrenched away from him. Her lips parted.

"It was a mistake," he blurted before she could change "okay" to "no freaking way." "Won't happen again. I— I just got excited about, ah, Michael and...everything." He took a deep breath and made a promise he didn't want to keep. "I won't touch you again, Dani. Hell, I won't even ask any personal questions. You have my word."

Without looking at him, Dani nodded, then hurried out of the room.

He wanted to follow her, to shoulder her aside when she got to Michael's crib.

Liar. You want to take her in your arms again. Inhale her scent of flowers and woman. Invade her mouth. Learn her body with your hands, your mouth, your—

Josh growled. His reactions to Dani's femininity had to stop. He didn't want any complications. He wanted Michael.

And if he didn't get stupid again, he could have that wonderful baby for the next six weeks.

Which reminded him... Josh spun around, looking for his boots, his wallet, Ravjani's keys. He had a few things to accomplish by tomorrow morning. Like, buy a car. Contact Marletta. He'd offer her an extra week's paid vacation if she turned one of his spare bedrooms into a nursery by the time they arrived.

As he stuffed his feet into his boots, Josh continued building his action list. Get a map. Work out an itinerary that wasn't too hard on a newborn and a new mom. Purchase a car seat. No, *the best* car seat made.

After dashing into Dani's room and practically throwing lunch at her, Josh headed out to arrange transportation. Stumbled over, then grinned at his jeans lying in the middle of the floor. *Oh, yeah. Gotta pack, too.*

Then, at the door, Josh thought of one more thing to do before tomorrow morning.

He was going to call his sister-in-law in Montana. Tell her he was taking her advice. Tell her it was damned good advice, too.

For the first time in years he was too busy to pick at his scab—and it was healing. *He* was healing.

Josh heard himself whistling as he climbed into Ravjani's ten-year-old car and jammed the key into the ignition. He'd get a new van, he decided. A plush, luxury-packed model. Something with plenty of room for Dani to rest while he drove her and Michael home. Although he didn't want her to recuperate *too* quickly....

The next morning when Josh showed off his purchase, Dani didn't know whether to laugh or cry. "How, how... Where..." She waved a hand weakly at the vehicle, a station wagon from the early seventies, its full coat of rust interspersed with remnants of white paint.

Josh shrugged awkwardly, if shoulders that magnificent

could actually look awkward. "Vern didn't have a great selection to choose from. But you wanted to leave today and it runs," he added defensively, so Dani murmured something approving and started to load Michael's things into the back.

"I'll do it!" Josh cried, snatching them out of her hands.

Dani went back into the motel room and nursed Michael while Josh packed the car and installed the baby seat he'd bought.

They were just finishing when Josh announced that everything was ready to go. Before she could stop him, he changed Michael's diaper, burped him and handed him back with a grin that sent her pulse skyrocketing. Then he escorted her to the car and strode away to the office to pay their bill.

How long am I going to be a burden to this man? Dani wondered three days later as she settled Michael in the car seat after lunch. There must be something I can do to express my gratitude for his kindness, she thought. But what?

Dani sighed. Josh Walker did everything superbly.

As he slid into the driver's seat and cranked the engine, she recalled the explanation he'd given for his willingness to help her and Michael. His narrow focus and the raw anger she'd heard so clearly in his voice— Dani smiled ruefully. Josh even did denial perfectly.

Like most people, when reality was too painful, he just didn't face it.

At the sound of paper being crumpled and tossed onto the dash, Dani smothered a laugh. *Or pick up after himself— at least, on the road.* Each morning, their departure was delayed while Josh searched through the rubble of his room for a shirt, his wallet, socks, or the car keys. Every evening, she practically needed a shovel to clean out the debris accumulated during the day's travel.

He apparently didn't know diddly about cars, either.

She'd fixed the radiator hose, a hundred miles out of No Lake, with a nickel's worth of duct tape. Fashioned a gas tank cap from a soda can when he forgot to replace it after filling up just east of Texarkana. And now...

Dani raised her head from the pillows. "Josh."

He didn't even look around. "You're supposed to be asleep."

She turned in time to see Josh smile over at the infant napping in his car seat. "Like Michael."

She ground her teeth. Yes, that's exactly how he treated her: like another baby to be wrapped in cotton wool and pampered. He insisted she spend half of every afternoon resting on the air mattress he'd put in the back of the wagon. Which was why she was lying here watching blue smoke pouring from the exhaust and billowing up around the rear of the car.

"How far to the next town?" she asked, trying to keep irritation out of her voice. The car was old and hadn't been well maintained, but there was no need to torture it to death!

Josh chuckled, a deep sound as smooth as heavy cream. "What do we need to stop for this time? A rest room?" He picked up the map and held it against the steering wheel. "There should be someplace in about ten minutes. Can you wait that long?"

Why, the patronizing— "You'd better hope your engine block can," she snapped. "You're burning so much oil, I expect the Red Adair folks to show up any minute."

Oh, dear. Dani held her breath. Would Josh blow up the way Jimmy used to every time somebody questioned his actions?

"Red who?" Josh asked. "What are you talking about?"

Dani listened carefully, but all she heard in his voice was mild interest. "This car has a leak," she explained. "That dark smoke means it's gotten worse. If we don't fix it, the car won't run. Ever again."

"Should I drive slower? Faster? I don't know a damned

thing about cars," Josh confessed genially. "My younger brother Dan is the mechanical one." He watched her reaction to that leading statement in the rearview mirror. Shoot. No curiosity that he could see. He'd been regretting that impulsive promise since he'd made it.

He kept hoping he'd stumble on something to make her change the rules. In the past three days he'd discovered a few thousand things about Dani Caldwell that he was dying to know.

"Keep going," she said. "When we reach the next town, find a store that sells—"

"Don't you mean a garage?" he asked, then practically groaned at the way her green eyes danced with mischief. No wonder she'd married right out of high school.

"We don't need a garage." She sounded supremely confident. "I can fix it with a rubber band and some instant nail glue."

And she did, crawling under the car right there in the parking lot.

He would have felt ridiculous just standing around—except that he got to hold Michael and show him his first elm tree while Dani worked. And he was busy revising his opinion of Dani Caldwell.

Not an angel. Young, but not a kid.

And not the kind of woman he'd ever known before.

The idea swept over Josh like a tidal wave over a rowboat as he stood there murmuring nonsense to Michael. He wasn't going to do anything stupid, but...maybe he could try being friends with the mother of this baby.

"That ought to do it," she said, emerging from beneath the chassis and wiping her hands on the towel Josh provided. "Now we just top off the oil and—"

"Oh, what an adorable baby!" exclaimed a white-haired lady as she passed the vehicle on her way to the store. Pausing to pat Michael's arm, the woman looked at Josh and smiled. "Looks just like his father," she said before continuing on her way.

Michael cooed. Dani finished wiping her hands, then folded the towel carefully.

"Does he?" Josh asked finally, his heart thudding in his chest. "I know I promised not to ask any personal questions, but...*does* Michael look like his father?"

At first she wasn't going to answer. *It's just your blond hair, I'll say, and change the subject.* But she'd never known a man like Josh: he took care of people without trying to control them, respected a person's strengths without becoming dependent on them. He deserved a real answer.

And as she looked into his azure eyes, she thought about the "accidental" pregnancy that still haunted him and the raw anguish he tried to hide when he announced, *I'm not married.*

If it took honesty to free Josh from the past, Dani decided, then that's how she'd repay him for his kindness and generosity. She'd certainly be gifting somebody's future—this man just had to become a full-time father to his own brood of kids!

"I think we're past the polite strangers stage, Josh. And actually, Michael looks a lot like I did as a baby," she added, squashing an intense longing as it formed.

"Then he's going to be one beautiful adult," Josh murmured, closing the distance between them.

"Okay, now it's my turn," she declared, desperate to halt...well, whatever was happening between them. Michael needed his mother's full attention.

Josh stepped back. Tightened his hold on the baby. "Okay, ask," he said eventually, his eyes wary. The breeze loosened a strand of his honey-gold hair and dropped it over one eyebrow. He left it there.

Dani took a deep breath and looked down again, wondering if she could scrape up courage from the pavement.

She was taking a risk, she supposed, of being stranded in Tennessee. But suddenly she didn't care.

She'd bet every dream she'd ever had that he was wrong about Carrie doing what she did out of ambition. No woman made that decision easily.

But the important point was simple.

That blame game of his was masking something else—guilt or fear or grief. Until it came to the surface and he dealt with it, the wounds he'd suffered would never heal. And if he couldn't do it by himself, maybe a kid from Lufkin—who'd learned her lessons the hard way, too—could help.

"Well? Go ahead, Dani. Ask," Josh said tonelessly. Ha. As if hiding feelings made them disappear.

"All right," she said, raising her eyes to meet his. "Back there in law school, did *you* know how babies get started?"

Chapter Four

"**O**f course I knew!" Knew—and even now, in the grip of intense fury, wanted to demonstrate with this petite Texas angel trying to play devil's advocate.

"Then what happened wasn't an accident. You—"

"Don't even *try* to go there, lady," Josh rasped. "I'm the lawyer, remember? The bottom line is that Carrie should ha—"

"No." Dani lifted Michael out of Josh's arms, settled the baby against her shoulder and began patting him rhythmically. "*You* should have."

Josh knew he looked stupid just standing there, goggle-eyed, but— "Are you saying that what she did was okay?"

"No. Oh, no." Something fierce in Dani's eyes cut into his self-righteous indignation like a hot sword through snow. "All I'm saying is that if *you'd* behaved responsibly at the beginning, she wouldn't have faced such a terrible decision."

Silence filled the parking lot. The town. The whole freaking state.

Damn her! *Don't pick at the scab,* Annie said. Well, Dani

Caldwell had just ripped it right off. And he was bleeding, like the loser in a gangland shoot-out.

She's missed the point, he told himself, struggling to stop the bleeding.

"I-if you've changed your mind about—" Dani shifted the baby higher as she licked her lips, trying not very successfully to hide terror behind bravado. "About taking us with you to Virginia, I understand. Just let me get Michael's things…"

Josh stared at her, shaken to the core. Did she really believe he'd just strand her here? How big a jerk did she think he was?

"Get in the car," he ordered through gritted teeth, then slammed around to the driver's side without waiting to see if she complied. Damn, damn, damn her!

All the way across Tennessee, Dani's accusation—and *her* reaction to *his* reaction—kept whispering through Josh's mind.

Even now, waking suddenly in the post-midnight silence, blinking at the green-neon light oozing past the curtains of his no-frills motel room from the twenty-four-hour truck stop sign across the road, Josh felt more ashamed than angry.

With a sigh, he abandoned sleep and sat up, rubbing his hand wearily over his unshaven jaw. He knew where Dani's questions were trying to lead him.

Dammit, even if he pleaded guilty to a kid's stupid disregard for consequences, two wrongs didn't make what Carrie did right. Discussing the past wasn't going to change it—or how he felt about it. Carrie's unilateral decision had robbed him of a man's most precious experience.

And Dani's giving it back to you.

Josh punched the rubbery pillow, automatically listening for sounds from the next room. He should have just kept his mouth shut. He'd done it for six long years—what was a few more? Besides, expecting understanding from a woman like Dani....

Oh, yeah, chimed a sanctimonious little voice in his head that sounded a hell of a lot like his sister-in-law. *A young widow with a fatherless newborn wouldn't know anything about surviving grief, pain and loss, would she?*

Okay, so maybe Dani could give him some pointers about moving on.

If that's where he wanted to go.

Josh hit the pillow again.

What if there's nothing there but more emptiness? Or another devastating heart wound?

Or a wife as brave and loving as Dani who'd be willing to give you a child of your own? He yanked the lump of polyester from beneath his head and flung it across the room.

A baby gurgle and faint crooning filtered through the motel wall.

Dammit, a woman like that would want his love, his heart. His soul, if he still had one. He wasn't sure he could give it. Wasn't willing to trust another woman with a piece of himself.

That's why he needed Dani's son. That adorable baby with his fuzzy halo of nearly transparent hair could fill the emptiness without any risk.

Not that he was a whole lot of fun yet. So far, Michael didn't do much besides eat, burp, and dirty diapers.

How long before he let them have a full night's sleep instead of brief lapses into unconsciousness?

He hoped Marletta had that nursery equipped. Maybe when the baby had his own room, he and Dani could get back to normal. That little scene this afternoon in the parking lot sure as hell hadn't been—

Once again he saw Dani's green eyes clouded with wariness as she leaped to erroneous—hell, downright insulting—conclusions.

He wanted to erase the shadows from those forest green eyes. Preferably with another kiss. One that exploded with passion enough to burn away her doubts and fears....

Folding his arms tightly across his chest, Josh tucked his hands deep into his armpits. That's why he was still here. In his own room, aching, rigid with longing, while Michael fussed and Dani stirred.

He hated missing even a minute with the baby, but tonight he'd let these broken mattress springs impale him in three— no, four—places. Because the idea of deepening his relationship with Dani Caldwell scared the writ out of him.

Josh closed his eyes, tipped his head back against the headboard. Face it. He didn't know diddly about women like Dani.

He worked with female attorneys, of course, but they were professional colleagues and that's how he treated them.

The only woman he ever really talked to was his secretary, Marletta. And she mostly nagged.

The select few he'd taken to bed, well... They weren't anything like Dani Caldwell. More worldly, more sophisticated—okay, jaded maybe—but they understood the rules. And talking was never a big part of the...interaction.

A vision of Dani formed in the darkness behind Josh's eyelids. Dani with him. Beneath him. Long legs tangled in silk sheets, her full breasts thrusting upward, begging for his mouth....

Josh groaned. His body clamored for her every waking second. Had from the minute he'd looked up through the starred windshield and seen a green-eyed angel.

But if he tried for something more than they'd agreed to, and failed at it, he risked losing his baby.

Josh groaned again.

That was the real flaw with secondhand fatherhood, with temporary parenting. Michael was somebody else's baby. Dani could leave, take him away anytime she wanted. She could be packing right this minute, folding the little shirts they'd bought yesterday—the ones with the tiny teddy bears all over and those itsy-bitsy snaps he could hardly fasten with his big hands....

No! Josh leaped off the bed, heading for the connecting door. Damned if he'd let her— He tripped over a boot. Staggered. Stomped his instep on the sole of the other boot, which for some reason was lying on its side in the middle of the floor next to his stupid jeans. *They* twined themselves around his ankles and he fell backward, smashing his funny bone into the nightstand before collapsing onto the mattress.

"Oow, sh—" Quickly, he muzzled the curse. Rubbed his damned elbow. Closed his eyes against the neon-tinged darkness. And made a decision. He *was* going to get past Carrie's betrayal and see if that made personal, permanent fatherhood possible.

Josh smirked into the motel silence. He knew how to go about moving on, too.

Find someone... Done.

Help them...

Whatever concessions he ended up agreeing to, Dani had to let him keep Michael for the full six weeks. That was nonnegotiable.

And maybe he'd see if he could remove some of the shadows from her eyes.

"Josh?" Her soft whisper reached him the same time her scent—that erotic mix of flowers, womanly sweetness and baby spit-up—did. "Are you okay?"

Hell, no. Actually, he realized, he was strenuously aroused. The pajama bottoms he'd bought to be presentable for Michael's feedings didn't hide the fact. They couldn't. Steel plating couldn't.

Josh scrambled for the covers, yanking them into a wad over his lap just as Dani clicked on the bedside lamp. She wore a thin cotton nightgown with the top three or four buttons undone. He pulled more covers over his growing...er, lap.

Then Dani leaned over him. At the right angle.

With the wrong expression. Her eyes were dark with concern, not glazed with passion. Still, her hair hung loose, a river of frothing maple-colored silk, streaming over her shoulders and down, down, down, almost touching his—

Josh groaned again with the effort required to keep his hands from reaching for her. Pulling her down on the bed. Cupping her breasts, taking their weight in his palms. Then rolling her under him. Taking her mouth in another glorious mating kiss while the universe exploded around them....

"Are you sick? In pain? Dizzy?" Genuine concern edged the questions.

Thank God. She did feel something besides wariness for him. Tension uncoiled deep inside and he smiled up at her through a haze of intense desire. *Ah, Dani,* his mind whispered. *Please. Touch me.*

Her hand floated toward him...hovered...then came down flat against his forehead. "Hmm. You don't feel hot," she announced after a second or two.

He almost choked. Not hot? He was on fire! If she moved that soft, little hand a few feet southward, she'd discover just how—Josh gritted his teeth as he fought for control—*stupid he was.*

He'd vowed six years ago never to be at the mercy of a woman again. Second chance or not, he wasn't ready to break that vow. Not yet. Not even with Dani Caldwell.

Even though she tempted him to the very edge of his limits.

Well, he'd just look for a way to spend time alone with Michael. And he'd control his desire for Michael's mother. No sweat. No problem. He'd prove it right now.

"I'm fine," he muttered, turning his head away. Instead of taking the hint, the fool woman slid her cool fingers down and around the side of his neck until the palm of her hand pressed against the base of his skull.

And he knew he was just kidding himself.

If, with the slightest pressure, she urged him upward to take her kiss, he'd do it. In a heartbeat. With pleasure aforethought and no holds barred. Ravage her mouth willingly and then do anything she wanted. Tell her anything she wanted. Give her anything she wanted.

Except my heart or my trust, Josh reminded himself fiercely. He couldn't give her that. Carrie's betrayal had taught him a lesson he couldn't unlearn overnight—even if he wanted to.

"No," she said as she moved away from the bed. "No fever. Is your vision blurred?"

Josh shook his head.

Dammit, he didn't want to keep wanting her like this. But he did.

"I hit my funny bone on the—" He pried one hand loose from his shield of motel bed linen and waved at the shelf beside the bed.

"Oh." That soft Texas drawl of hers stroked over him like hot satin. She turned to leave. "I won't disturb you any longer."

Ha. As long as he had eyes and she was this side of the horizon, she was going to disturb him.

Still, he meant to let her go, but some part of him started harping on that near-death, second-chance stuff again, because she didn't retreat more than one step before he said, "No, wait, Dani. About this afternoon. I want to…apologize. For…"

For what? That was the crux of it. For refusing to forgive what Carrie did? For refusing to forget it?

No, no, never. "Ah-h-h…"

As she watched Josh struggle to smooth over the situation without compromising his beliefs, Dani knew she had to let him off the hook. After the years of Jimmy's escalating lies and broken promises, she respected, even admired Josh's integrity—whether she agreed with him or not.

"I'm the one who should apologize," she said truthfully,

toying with a strand of hair. Bitter experience had taught her that well-meaning efforts to change minds didn't change hearts—and without that... "Your life is none of my business."

"Well, I didn't have to bite your head off." Rueful regret turned his eyes the color of summer dusk. "Dani, please." His deep voice pulled at her. "Don't ever be afraid of me."

Against her will and every bit of sense she possessed, Dani's gaze slid down the strong, satiny column of the neck she'd touched just a moment ago to feast on Josh's magnificently male, gloriously muscled bare chest and the crinkly dark hair that swirled over and down... Heat coiled through her. Again.

The way it did every time she saw it. Or those incredible turquoise eyes. Or that deliciously dangerous dark stubble when he needed a shave. Or—

Okay. Her reaction to Josh Walker proved that motherhood hadn't completely replaced her womanly feelings. *Get over it.*

Dani sighed. She was too busy to indulge her femininity. Parenting a helpless infant wasn't quite as simple as she'd thought it would be.

Well, it *was* simple—feed, change, soothe to sleep.

But people said this was the easy part and, so far, the Queen of Coping felt completely overwhelmed. How was she going to handle the next eighteen years?

Love is all I have.

Unfortunately, child-rearing took money, too.

"You're safe with me, Dani." Josh's deep voice brought her back to the present.

Dani beamed at him gratefully. *Right...first things first. Get Michael out of diapers before worrying about paying for Harvard.*

Josh leaned forward, clenching the bedclothes with white-knuckled fists. "No matter what our differences, a Walker always keeps his promises, Dani. Trust me."

Heaven help her, she wanted to. Wanted to climb into bed next to him, too. Rest her head on his shoulder, press her lips against his smooth skin. Be taken to paradise with another of his— *Practiced kisses. Out of your league, sweetie,* she reminded herself. "Well, I'm sure obliged to you for…everything."

That's why, when she'd sensed the sorrow and guilt underneath his bitterness, she'd tried to help him release it. A man as patient and gentle as Josh should share children of his own with some lucky woman…but he'd made it clear he wasn't ready to face his own part in the tragedy that still held him prisoner.

So be it.

"Uh, Dani, about the other—"

"No." She held up her hand. "Don't."

"Don't?" Through the semidarkness, Josh's deep voice caressed her again and another tidal wave of longing swept over her. "Don't what, Dani?"

"Apologize for anything, especially your beliefs," she said, summoning a lopsided smile. "Let's just consider the subject closed."

He swung his feet out from under the covers and sat up. Rested his elbows on his hard, muscular thighs and thrust his fingers into his thick hair. "Maybe I can't," he said to the industrial carpet beside the bed. Not quite tonelessly.

Dani looked at the handsome, virile man sitting on the edge of the motel bed and saw the pain he was trying to hide—from himself as much as anyone.

For a moment Dani wondered if her motive was really selfless gratitude—or leftover wishes.

It didn't much matter.

She knew from her own past how tempting denial was. Knew, too, its inevitable failure. Accepting reality, however unpleasant, offered the only route past life's pain.

So show him the way and let him decide if he wants to take it. Then get on with your own life. And Michael's.

"I'm sorry, Josh, but it *is*," she said. Gently but firmly. "It's over. Your baby is gone. Your girlfriend..."

Josh's turquoise eyes flashed blue fire. "I would have married her!" he snapped. With a shrug, he dropped his head back into his hands.

"You know, I can't even remember what she looks like now," he confessed to his toes in a bemused tone before issuing a sigh that seemed to come from the same general region. "She didn't— Why didn't she tell me?" he asked in a half whisper.

And that was the question, of course, that still tormented him all these years later. Unfortunately, only Carrie could answer it.

The thought flitted through Dani's mind that Jimmy's parents—Michael's grandparents—might spend the rest of their lives asking the same thing about *her*.

Okay, when she felt stronger and more secure, she'd figure out a safe way to let them know they had a grandson. Right now—

"I have no idea, Josh," she admitted. "If you'd talked about spending the rest of your lives together—"

"Rest of our lives?" Josh growled, scowling at her. "Hell, I was just trying to get through the semester!"

So. The devil riding him was guilt as well as grief. Wrapping her arms around her middle, Dani said a silent prayer that she wouldn't have to gather up Michael and start a new life at 3:00 a.m. in— She realized she didn't know where they were exactly.

Except maybe on the brink of a breakthrough. "Then why were you having unprotected sex with her?" she asked quietly. "Were you ready for a baby?"

Josh leaped off the bed. Even from ten feet away, he seemed to tower over her. "No!" he shouted, then lowered his voice with a glance toward the connecting door that led to Michael. "Okay. No," he repeated grimly. "I wasn't. But I would have gotten ready."

"Some people—" *like Jimmy* "—can't just 'get ready.'"

"Are you excusing her?" he asked, disbelief vibrating through every soft-spoken word.

"No." Dani shook her head adamantly. "Accepting."

"Never."

He'd stood by her during Michael's delivery, when he wanted to be anywhere else on earth. The world needed all the wonderful fathers it could get. So she gave it one last shot. "You don't have to like it, just—"

"Well, I don't." Every line of his muscular body went to granite mode as he sliced off the phrase. "I won't."

Been there. Great way to waste a lifetime. Dani lifted her chin. "And what does your attitude achieve, Josh? Does it change the past?" She answered her own question. "No. It just destroys the future, too."

She looked down at the floor, then let him see the pain of her own shattered dreams. "If it's any help," she said with a sad smile, "I can assure you, from personal experience, a baby isn't enough to glue a shaky relationship together."

After a moment of utter stillness Josh extended his hands in a way that made her want to walk right into his arms and seek comfort in the most elemental way a man and a woman could give and receive it.

And then she *was* in his arms.

And he held her wordlessly, held her tight, pressing his cheek against the top of her head.

It felt so right.

She felt so right. So safe.

In the most dangerous place she could be. A place where dreams could grow again. They weren't big dreams: a home, a family, a loving husband who cherished her the way she cared for him....

Darn Josh Walker, anyway. He made her want things she shouldn't. Another moment of heaven in his arms. Another bone-melting kiss. The right to thrust *her* fingers into that thick, silky, golden hair.

Don't be a fool, she warned herself. *Your life belongs to Michael now. And so does your heart.*

She stepped back and he let her go. She forced her feet to turn toward her own room.

Still—she couldn't help hoping the seed she'd planted took root.

Because Josh deserved happiness. Everyone did, of course, but he'd been grieving for years.

"Dani." His voice stopped her in the doorway. "I don't want to argue with you. But what Carrie did was wrong. Forgiveness doesn't change that."

Oooh—arrogant idiot! "That's what I've been trying to tell you," she retorted without turning around. "It's not about forgiveness."

Somehow she got herself back into her room and the door closed behind her.

K-I-S-S. Keep it simple, stupid. Take care of Michael. Get your strength back. Come up with some viable way to support yourself—and get out of Josh Walker's life before your heart makes any fatal mistakes.

Clearly the man needed a woman's touch, some gentle guidance back to the land of the living.

Just as clearly, she wasn't the woman. She'd failed once—to save her high school sweetheart from his self-destructive ways. She couldn't risk another failure, another heartbreak. She had a baby to raise. She needed all of her *self* for herself. For Michael.

Which put Josh Walker strictly off-limits.

Dani closed her eyes to get a few minutes' rest before Michael's next feeding. Teardrops formed behind her lashes. From long habit, she started to choke them back.

Oh, go ahead, she told herself, turning her face into the pillow and letting the tears run. *Even the Queen of Coping deserves an occasional night off.*

* * *

The distant whine of an eighteen-wheeler downshifting filtered into the room.

If it's not about forgiveness, what the hell is it about? Josh wondered with a frown as he crossed the room and retrieved the pillow. Slumping back on the bed, he crammed the lump behind his head and stared into the greenish darkness, waiting for the sun to come up, trying to figure out a way to reclaim whatever ground he'd lost tonight.

Because one thing glowed clearly through the murky motel air: he had to keep this baby. *This* baby. He'd never understand women enough to have a kid of his own. He needed time with Michael.

At dawn, Josh showered, did the shaving routine, dug around until he found a clean navy T-shirt, and got dressed. Listened to the sounds next door until, around six, he took a deep breath, then simply strode in there as if nothing had happened and muscled Dani aside to burp and diaper Michael. As he settled the baby in the carrier, he urged Dani to go over to the truck stop and order breakfast.

"Food's usually pretty good in those places," he said gruffly, not quite meeting her gaze. "Thought maybe you'd enjoy a few minutes to yourself. Michael can stay with me while I pack."

After chewing on her lip for a few seconds, Dani nodded. "Okay, I'll save you a seat."

When the door closed behind her, Josh carried Michael carefully into his room, placed the carrier in the center of the bed and turned on the TV. Then he snatched up the phone.

Punched in his calling card sequence and Marletta's home number so fast he expected the touch-pads to melt. Tapped his foot impatiently while he waited for the connection. Reached over to touch Michael's cheek and grinned with pure pleasure—just as his call was answered.

"Who*ever* this is, you'd better have a *real* good reason for calling so early," Marletta warned his ear.

Josh chuckled. "Don't dis me, woman—I happen to know you leave for church in thirty minutes."

Laughter with a Georgia accent flowed through the receiver.

"So, do I owe you some extra vacation?" he asked.

"You shore do!" Marletta claimed to be one-quarter Cherokee and mostly African-American—with a couple of Welsh immigrants thrown in just for fun. Her skin was the color of café latte, her temper as hot as a habañero pepper, but her accent was pure Southern drawl.

She was also sharper than a steel razor, a black belt busybody and the world's biggest marshmallow beneath her bristly exterior. She'd been with Josh since he opened his practice, laid rightful claim to half the credit for his success and was probably the closest thing he had to a friend.

"You got everything?" Josh glanced at his watch impatiently. He wanted to channel-hop with his baby for a couple of minutes before joining Dani at the diner.

"Your credit card company loves you, Walker," Marletta assured him dryly. "I tried my best to buy one of everything Baby City sells. From crib to playpen to changing table—right on down to the Mommy's Listening Post intercom deal and a windup bunny mobile. Oh, and a rocking chair. So when do I get to meet the reason for this frenzied shopping spree?"

Josh leaned over to press a kiss on his baby's soft fuzzy head. "His mother won't let him out of her sight for more than a few minutes just yet."

"She's the one I want to meet, you dingdong."

"Well, uh, she…she's pretty wiped out." *When she's not wiping the floor with me.* One of these days, when he could reason coolly around the little angel hellion with the Texas accent, he intended to revisit that forgiveness crap and show her the holes in her argument, but— "I don't think she's up for visitors, yet, Marletta."

"She's not suffering postpartum depression, is she?"

Please, no. He'd be worse than useless trying to cope with rampaging female emotions. "Uh, how would I tell if she's got that?" he asked cautiously.

"Well, is she teary-like? Uninterested in the baby?"

"Dani?" Josh gave his heart permission to start beating again. "Nah, she's devoted to Michael." He looked over at the little miracle whose entrance into this world he'd witnessed. "Marletta, do you know how incredible babies are?" he asked, astonished again. In love again.

"*And* how much work they are! Now, listen. No matter how much she loves her baby, your Dani's bound to be feeling overwhelmed right now. She needs emotional support and you're elected." That was Marletta. As subtle as a pickax.

"The lady doesn't need anything from me."

At least, nothing I could give her. I admire her courage and devotion. And I sure as hell lust for her body. But that's the most I can offer a woman.

Because it is *about forgiveness. Isn't it?*

"A cheerful little bouquet wouldn't kill you," Marletta snapped.

Josh reverted to a safer subject. "Well, thanks for maxing out the plastic, Marletta," he said. "I'll call ya when we're back in the 'hood," he added with a smirk.

"Check it out, kiddo," he said a moment later, mashing the remote with one hand as he scooped clothes from various surfaces with the other. "Television." After stuffing garments and toiletries haphazardly into the shopping bag he was using as a suitcase, he snagged the carrier and headed for the diner. "Hey, when we get home, we'll surf the Net together."

Home. Almost there.

Not that the town house was a mansion or anything, but it was a hell of an improvement over that pathetic cabin Dani had been living in when she'd fished him out of that flash flood.

And given him another chance.

Okay. He still blamed Carrie, but... After last night's frank discussion, the fire of his anger didn't burn quite as hot today. And he had Dani to thank for it.

What the hell, maybe he'd buy her some damned flowers, after all.

Josh crossed the last few feet of graveled parking lot with two brisk strides. Yanked open the diner's door. Hit a wall of sound and smell. Clattering cutlery, clinking china and loud country music. Cigarette smoke, fried eggs, strong coffee.

Standing near the door, Josh scanned the counter, the tables scattered across the black-and-white linoleum floor, then the booths to his right. No Dani. He looked to the left.

A mountainous trucker with a greasy ponytail sat in the first booth, his mile-wide back blocking the view of the booths along that side of the diner.

Holding Michael steady, Josh started to move past the mountain.

"N-no thanks. I'm waiting for someone." The familiar voice sounded calm. Stoic, even. But her green eyes were dark with shadows.

"Come on, baby." The big trucker reached across the table. Dani shrank away from him. "It ain't gonna hurt ya to be a little friendly like."

Josh gripped the baby carrier's handle hard enough to pulverize it. "Get your hands off her," he snarled as a red, unreasoning haze exploded around him. *She's mine—my woman!* "Now!"

The trucker didn't bother to look up. "In the first place, I ain't touched her," he said in a rough, aggressive voice. "An' in the second place, why don't you just mind yore own business, buddy?"

"I am," Josh said through gritted teeth. "The lady's with me."

Time slowed to a crawl: nothing happened right away.

Then with a grunt, the trucker placed ham-size hands flat on the tabletop and began extracting himself from the booth. Eventually, he clawed his way free and stood.

For the second time in a week, Josh found himself facing death.

This time, it stood six-eight. Weighed a solid two-seventy, two-eighty. And its name was Bubba.

Chapter Five

At least, that's what the name patch on the shirt said.

Not that Josh gave a damn. "The lady's with me," he repeated, setting Michael's carrier carefully on the booth bench next to Dani as the primitive red haze pulsated around him like a nuclear blast wave.

Vaguely, in the background, he heard tables being pushed aside as people scrambled out of the way. The steel guitar wailing from the jukebox fell silent in mid-twang.

Great. An audience.

Bubba shuffled a step closer, forcing Josh to look upward in order to meet the big jerk's stare.

Brilliant, Walker. First fight since high school and you pick Paul Bunyan as your opponent.

Didn't matter. As long as he could stand, crawl or move, no man was going to bother his...*Dani.*

Josh braced himself, feet spread, weight balanced.

"I don't see no ring says so," the giant declared, running a huge paw over his head and out to the end of his ponytail. "An' I don't like your attitude," he added, raising both hands and forming fists in front of his acre-wide chest. Scarred-knuckle, softball-size fists.

Dani cleared her throat. ''Now, Josh. And, er, Bubba. I'm sure ther—''

''Get out of the booth, Dani,'' Josh commanded in a deep voice without taking his gaze from the mammoth trucker.

Automatically, she picked up Michael, scooted to the end of the bench, and scrambled to her feet. The two males ignored her. Too busy glaring at each other.

''You want to try changing it?'' Josh asked, baring his teeth at his opponent.

Bubba snarled back.

Dani chewed on her lip as the two men squared off—at dawn in a Virginia truck stop, for heaven's sake. Why, one punch from Bubba could put Josh right into intensive care.

She had to do something, but what?

Anything, silly. Just don't let that monster hurt Josh.

As she devised and discarded schemes a new knot formed in her stomach.

How could *she* teach a boy to be a man? Dani wondered while Josh and Bubba traded more glares.

Could she teach her son *this*—unhesitating courage to put himself at risk in defense of those weaker?

Well, plenty of single women did a perfectly adequate job of raising sons, she reminded herself.

''Take Michael and wait outside,'' Josh rasped.

No way. Courage is one thing, senseless sacrifice to mayhem is another. ''Come on, guys. There's no need to—''

Both men growled her to a halt, then proceeded with their male posturing as if they'd never been interrupted.

''I just might decide to,'' Bubba informed Josh.

''You're welcome to try,'' Josh retorted.

They were toe-to-toe now. Josh, a granite-jawed Viking looking for someplace to pillage. Bubba, a gargantuan wrestling maniac. The only things missing were makeup and tights.

"Look, buddy, why'nt ya ask the lady what—''

"I don't need to ask the lady anything," Josh snapped.

That made Dani growl!

The two men started circling each other, bobbing their shoulders, shuffling their feet, waving their fists in tight, menacing little circles.

Oh, this is ridiculous. Dani pushed her way between the two idiots. As she hoped, her unexpected action seemed to snap the macho morons out of their testosterone trance for a second.

Now, keep them off balance long enough for their brains to start working again. If either one of them had any functional cells left between his ears.

Mentally crossing her fingers, Dani took a deep breath, pictured one of those girls who give out auto racing trophies and...giggled.

Josh and the mountainous trucker froze.

"Now, honey, I'm sure the man didn't mean any harm," she said, forcing out another giggle and swatting Josh's arm playfully. "Besides—you know you shouldn't tussle with civilians."

Turning to Bubba with a bimbo-ish smile, she confided, "'Cuz it just wouldn't be fair, see? Why, my Josh can kill a man half a dozen ways—" she snapped her fingers "—with nothin' more than his hands."

Ha. Beneath his multihued tattoos, Bubba went pale. His eyes began shifting, looking for escape. With a quick, silent prayer, Dani showed him the exit sign.

"Really. Don't pay him any mind," she advised the colossal trucker in a heart-o'-Texas drawl. "He's just testy these days because—" Flashing another sassy smile, she lifted the carrier to show off Michael. "I had the baby a week ago and he's not...well, you know...gettin' any..."

And then, by God, she winked at the behemoth. Winked! Josh felt his mouth fall open.

Slowly the trucker looked from Dani to Josh, who remained balanced on the balls of his feet, red haze still simmering behind his eyeballs.

Like a *dolt*. Dani didn't need his protection.

Hell, she was going to get both of them out of this. *Without a mark on us.*

Which, he decided wryly, was fine with him. Otherwise, his could have been the shortest second chance in history.

As his adrenaline rush slowed to a trickle and the last of the crazed fury that had possessed him the second he'd seen fear shadowing Dani's eyes drained away, Josh let his fists drop to his sides.

Bubba's lips quivered, then his mouth split open—and a guffaw emerged. A ham of a hand slapped Josh's shoulder, practically sending him sailing across the diner.

"Well, ol' buddy," he boomed in a jovial voice, antagonism instantly exchanged for male solidarity. "I ken see why you're on edge. But cheer up," he advised. "Ya gotta a fine-lookin' kid there, an' yore ol' lady won't be outta commission forever." He guffawed again. Slapped Josh's shoulder again.

"Josh."

Lordy, the way she caressed his name—he lost all interest in Bubba.

Then the darned woman handed him Michael. *Well, hell. Checkmate. She knew he couldn't fight the giant one-handed....*

"Come on, honey," Dani said, her green eyes pleading. Heat radiated from her fingers touching his arm. The warmth spread through him, seeking—and arousing—every masculine cell he had. "Let's go."

"Okay," he conceded, then swore under his breath when Bubba guffawed again.

Two could play this game, Josh decided, sliding his free hand under Dani's braid. "Whatever you want, sweetheart," he murmured, then pulled her into a skintight embrace. Kissed her swiftly. Hotly. Thoroughly.

He staggered a little when he let her go.

But so did she, he noted with a certain grim satisfaction.

Then Josh gave Bubba a comradely nod and guided Dani out of the diner with a proprietary hand on the small of her back. Hustled her across the parking lot, the street and right to the car.

Without a word.

Well, he was busy reeling. Again.

And revising his game plan. Again. Because discretion was the better part of valor, after all. Dani Caldwell's kisses rocked him from one end of his manhood to the other. They made him tremble with need.

Dammit, right now, *right here,* he burned to thrust his fingers deep into that glorious hair, pull her close and kiss the living daylights out of her again, then slide his hands along the smooth curve of her hips, up over her rib cage and around to claim her full breasts. Until—when *she* was trembling with need, too, he'd take her into one of those motel rooms they'd so recently occupied—

With Michael. Week-old *Michael.*

Dammit! What was wrong with him?

He had to stop thinking that Dani wasn't like other women. Had to stop kissing her. Wanting her. All the time. In any position. *Especially with her on top, her hair loose and falling like silk over his—*

He'd learned the hard way the dangers of giving a woman access to his heart, so how could he go all possessive over one he'd only known a week?

He couldn't. He wouldn't.

He just had.

Temporary insanity. That was the only explanation.

Josh jerked his hand from her back. Clamped it on the door handle and yanked.

He didn't trust himself to say anything, so he didn't. Just motioned her into the car. Fastened Michael carefully in the back seat.

And drove out of that godforsaken little town as if the wisps of morning mist were angry ghosts hell-bent on pursuing him.

They'd made a bargain, dammit. Six weeks of sanctuary for her; six weeks of Michael for him. He had to shake this feverish desire for Dani or he was no better than Bubba.

So, he'd take her and Michael home and get them settled, then barricade himself in the office for a week or two. Slide back into his routine. His safe, sterile, *empty* routine.

It wasn't much of a life change for a man with a second chance.

But he wasn't putting any more shadows in those green eyes.

And by the time he got a grip on his rampant desire, maybe Michael would be more fun, too. See? Win-win. Except that he felt more lost than ever, dammit.

A Walker keeps his promises. Josh tightened his hands on the steering wheel, pressed the accelerator—and kept driving.

Dani stared through the car window as they passed neatly plowed fields tucked in narrow valleys, climbed through wooded hills toward the rocky outcroppings that lay like spines along their crests. She studied the dogwood trees whose blooms floated like pink and white clouds of butterflies through the forests.

Virginia looked like East Texas, only more beautiful. She'd feel comfortable here, if only…

She glanced over at Josh, who drove competently, but silently. Nursing his bruised male ego, probably, because she stepped in before he could punch somebody silly.

Against her will, her gaze dropped to his strong hands wrapped around the steering wheel. They'd formed fists ready to defend and protect her, yet they could hold Michael as gently as a snowflake.

She wondered how they'd touch a woman. Tenderly? Hungrily?

Demanding passion and giving it at the same, incredible time?

A tremor of longing swept through her. She'd never known that kind of touch. In the beginning Jimmy had been sweet, but urgent and fumbling. In the last two years, at increasingly longer intervals, he'd simply gone through the motions. Distracted. Disinterested.

Somehow, Dani didn't think Josh Walker let anything distract him when he made love to a woman.

Memories of that exquisite kiss moments ago led to fantasies of that golden head bent over her, those firm lips searching, exploring…those hands caressing—

Oh, stop dreaming! You're not the kind of woman Josh would be interested in. You're just a kid from Lufkin, Dani reminded herself as she shifted on the seat. *A kid with a kid.*

As if to say amen to that, Josh growled.

She glanced sideways at her scowling companion.

Automatically, her gaze slid to Michael. Her son—who would surely benefit from having a father. Unfortunately, she didn't know how to supply one without ending up with a husband.

Dani chewed on her lip. She'd always wanted a home and a big, loving family, but after the disillusionment of her marriage, she wasn't sure she wanted another husband.

Unless he has honey-gold hair and turquoise eyes, unflinching courage and a kind heart hidden beneath that gruff exterior.

This particular model also has a big old chip of guilt and resentment on his shoulder, Dani reminded herself with a sigh, wishing there was some way she could help him let go of his past. But what could she say? How could she convince him to open his heart when she was afraid to do so herself?

Would demonstration prove more effective than speeches?

Her insides shivered with anxiety—and sudden anticipation.

Josh growled again and Dani gladly abandoned future difficulty for present certainty. "Huh," she said, crossing her arms under her breasts. "I thought so. You *are* angry."

"What?"

"Look—I'm sorry," she exclaimed, spreading her hands, palms up. "I didn't know what else to do. If he hadn't been the size of Vermont, I would have stayed out of it, I swear."

After a moment of granite-jawed silence, Josh chuckled.

A sound as rich as butterscotch. It ought to be illegal, Dani thought wryly, wishing she could hear it more often—until she remembered that her wishes should be saved for Michael.

Josh showed a flash of white teeth. "Believe me, Dani, I'm glad you jumped in."

"Really?"

She'd never met a man like Josh Walker. Seeing a woman in danger, he'd put himself at risk without hesitation. Now he twinkled those turquoise eyes at her and thanked her for interfering?

Another cream-smooth chuckle. "Oh, yeah. I prefer survival any day over getting the smithereens beaten out of me just to demonstrate my manhood."

Images of the magnificent male form she'd undressed flitted through her head, melted her insides. Roused all her longings....

"You don't need to demonstrate it," she blurted. "Anyone can see— Oh, you know what I mean," she finished lamely.

"Thanks for the endorsement," he replied with a gleam in his azure eyes. When he smiled, that deep coiling heat seared through her. Tempted her to dream again, to try again, to love again.

Hey—reality check on aisle three! There is, there can be

nothing between you and Josh Walker. Except Michael. For five more weeks.

"Well, anyway, thanks for standing up for me," Dani said.

"I'd have done the same for any woman," Josh insisted. Ha. What a liar he'd become! Under oath, the truth was that nobility had nothing to do with it. He'd simply gone nuts when he'd seen that creep reaching for Dani.

And now, an hour later, he was still nuts. Still fighting a pulsating desire to possess this Texas angel himself.

Visions of her lying naked in passion-tangled sheets danced back and forth across his brain like a high-kick chorus line.

Chill, man, he ordered himself. *Douse the fire of these damned, inappropriate feelings with cold facts.* "You're the one who saved my as—er, life," he said, before adding in silky, leading-the-witness tones, "Where did you learn how to defuse situations like that?"

She lifted, then lowered one shoulder. "Jimmy started spending too much time in the wrong places with the wrong people."

She turned to look out the window and Josh divided his attention between the road and the maple-colored braid bisecting her back.

"Maybe I should have gone with him more," she whispered to the glass. "Maybe I could have done something...."

The pain in her voice was too damned familiar. Josh's first impulse was to change the subject, but— "Nobody can stop another person if they're hell-bent on self-destruction." *And wasn't that what Dani tried to tell you last night?* he asked himself. Then frowned. He still didn't see where nonforgiveness fit in, though.

Josh realized he'd have to think about it.

Later. *She's chewing on that lip again.* "If Michael cooperates," he said quickly, "we might make it to Fallsboro before his next feeding."

Turning to give him a grateful smile, she took the cue. "How long have you lived there?"

He had to think about that, too. Had he spent the past six years sleepwalking through life?

"Couple of years," he said finally. "I've been in the D.C. area nearly five."

"Why D.C.? I thought you grew up in Montana."

Damn, when her eyes glowed like priceless emeralds, free of those shadows of pain and sorrow, and she curved those lush lips in an encouraging smile like that, he'd tell her anything.

So, as the old station wagon chugged along, he divulged his hope to influence environmental law during the creation process. Heard himself gushing that he'd already provided information during hearings in the House and was currently trying to build rapport with the newly appointed chairman of an important senate committee.

So far, Elliston Perrodeaux remained elusive, Josh admitted with a lopsided grin, but he continued to call the senator's office regularly with invitations to meet for breakfast, lunch or dinner.

"One of these days, I'll catch him in a weak moment," he vowed with a wry chuckle. "Until then..." He shrugged modestly, then twisted around to check on Michael, who uncurled a finger as he slept.

Josh beamed. *Was this kid brilliant or what?*

"Tell me about Fallsboro," Dani suggested. "What's it like?"

"Well, it's, uh..." The place had a grocery store, a bank, a dry cleaner, but for all Josh knew, it could be populated by three-headed androids.

He pointed with relief. "Decide for yourself."

As he drove past the Welcome To Fallsboro sign, Dani looked around eagerly. So did he—seeing the town for the first time. Hmm. Nice. Clusters of houses. A little farmland. A small central area of thriving shops and offices. Good place to raise a kid.

For six weeks.

Dani fiddled with the end of her braid, then tossed it aside. "About us—me and Michael—staying at your house," she began, her cheeks flushing a delicate pink. "Are you sure it will be big enough?"

Josh swallowed a groan. The state of Montana wasn't big enough. But he was…*again.*

"Plenty of room," he proclaimed finally. "Three bedrooms, two baths. Kitchen. Garage." He couldn't remember any other details, like what color the carpet was or whether he owned any wallpaper.

"It sounds wonderful."

"Judge for yourself," Josh said, his jaw suddenly rocklike.

Dani peered eagerly through the windshield. They'd been driving past small, lovingly maintained older homes, their front yards edged with flowerbeds and sprinkled with toys and bikes. At the end of the street was a park, complete with swings and sandboxes, paths and playing fields. She blinked back sudden tears; this was one of the dreams she'd lost. "Wh-where? Which one's yours?"

"It's over there." Josh pointed past the park.

To a prison. Actually, it was a starkly new, gated "community" of identical brick buildings flanked by an army of light poles and a security fence. Upscale professionals would probably consider the place desirable, but to Dani it looked more like a correctional facility than a home.

There was even a guardhouse at the entrance.

As they paused there to fill out a guest form, Dani decided it was a fitting residence for Josh. He was, after all, still a prisoner of his own guilt and grief, doing hard time—alone.

Dani clasped her hands together in her lap and mechanically nodded to the security guard as Josh pulled the car through the entrance. Oh, how she wanted to heal his wounded heart. So he could have what he deserved and obviously desired: a wife to cherish, children to raise. A family to love.

But how? And why? For his sake, or to fulfill her own failed savior complex?

"Aa-wa-aa." The soft baby fuss came from the back seat.

Dani smiled. Thank heaven for easily solved problems. "Josh—"

"We're here." Two streets past the gate, they turned, then pulled into a short driveway. After running a hand over his jaw, Josh cut the engine, climbed out of the car, came around to Dani's side and helped her out before extracting Michael and his carrier from the back seat.

"Why don't you two go in and get started while I unpack the car? Just…let me find the house key," he said, handing the baby carrier to Dani and fishing in his pocket. With difficulty, of course, because, as usual, there wasn't much room right now….

No key, either.

Where was the stupid thing? Leaning into the car, Josh dug through the ashtray. Aha. Locating the ring of keys among the coins, gum wrappers and gas receipts, he handed it to her. "Here. The nursery's…" Hell, he'd forgotten to ask Marletta which room she'd set it up in. He tried to get away with a vague wave. "Upstairs."

Dani stared at him for a second, then lifted her chin and turned toward the town house. She'd been dismissed—and subtly notified that the closeness they'd enjoyed on their journey was over. Obviously, now that they were in Josh's home territory, he wanted to return to their original agreement.

Fine. We'll just be two strangers who happen to share a roof for a few weeks, she told herself as she carried the quietly fussing baby up the narrow sidewalk. Cool cordiality from Josh Walker would satisfy her completely.

Except for her silly heart, that couldn't seem to stop wanting something more—something she'd tasted in his sizzling, sweet kisses.

"Come on, Michael," Dani whispered as she turned the key in the lock. "Let's take a quick tour of our temporary residence and get you fed."

Slowly she opened the door and stepped inside a small, bare entry with a staircase hugging the wall on the right and a short hallway leading to a bright kitchen at the rear of the town home. On the left, an archway led to—

Crossing the black-and-white marble of the foyer, Dani gasped as she viewed Josh's living room.

A basketball rested atop a lampshade. Three—*three?*—athletic shoes draped with socks resided on various shelves of built-in bookcases that covered one wall. Stacks of video cassettes and CDs balanced on soda cans stood next to a computer in the far corner. At least a week's worth of newspapers drifted over an armchair, and the sofa held mounds of books, several shirts and a pair of sweatpants. An umbrella *and* a tennis racket sprouted from the crevasse between the seat cushion and the sofa back.

A TV sat on the coffee table, held in place by a set of barbells.

Either the place had been attacked by vandals or Josh Walker really was a full-time, certified slob, she decided with a grin. Thank heavens! Without a few flaws to make him human, who could resist him?

And Dani knew: letting herself fall in love with Josh would guarantee a heartache she couldn't afford. *So stay busy. Don't give your heart time to make that mistake.*

"Hmm. Making this place habitable would get my figure back in shape fast, too," she mused as she retreated to the foyer and headed for the stairs. "Now there's a million-dollar idea. Clean Your Way To Fitness."

Upstairs, a door on the right revealed a large room carpeted in clothes, more sporting goods and scads of books and folded-open magazines. "Master bedroom," Dani guessed with a giggle. How could such utter messiness yield such perfectly pristine masculine beauty?

Michael uttered a cry of definite frustration.

The nursery was across the hall from Josh's room, overlooking the front of the town home, and was fully furnished, as advertised. After peeking at the connecting bath and the bedroom beyond, Dani sank into a rocking chair near the room's window. Josh's nieces and nephews were lucky kids, she thought, eyeing the cheerful room and bright, lavish furnishings as she guided Michael to lunch.

Lucky to have uncles like Josh. Dani frowned. Unless she and Jimmy's parents made peace, her poor baby might never know his relatives.

Michael's hand began moving languidly, a signal he was full. Maybe Pete Caldwell's custody campaign was motivated by genuine concern for his grandson. But she still couldn't give up her baby.

Gently, she disengaged Michael and laid him in the crib. She'd just refastened her blouse when a velvety male voice purred across her shoulder, "How's my darling?"

Dani closed her eyes against the longing. The foolish longing.

To spin those dreams again, the ones she'd cherished and lost—of happily ever after in a home filled with laughter and love, of moonlight drifting across a bed and a man who loved her, turning...reaching for her.... And babies. More babies. With blond hair and turquoise eyes....

Oh, pooh. You're heading straight for trouble if you don't get a grip on this rampant romantic streak of yours.

She reckoned the man broke hearts by the baker's dozen. Couldn't even help it, probably. Look at him, thrusting those long fingers through that thick, silky gold hair. Standing so close she could smell his brisk, piney scent. Singeing her with his hot turquoise glance. Cocking his narrow hip as he lifted Michael from the bed and settled him against that broad shoulder.

Then flashing his patented sexy, lopsided smile.

"Listen Dani, I— That is, could you…" Josh swayed back and forth, patting Michael's back rhythmically, not meeting her eye.

Dani's heart started pounding. Had he changed his mind about giving them sanctuary? No, not Josh. He'd stayed with her during those long hours at Ravjani's clinic, stood up to Bubba. "Could I what?" she prompted finally.

"Well…I've been out of town awhile, so the cupboard's bare. And I hate shopping," he confessed with a shrug. "So I wondered if… Well—" Finally, he rushed to the point. "I'll stay with Michael if you'll go buy us some groceries." *Please, please, please.*

She just blinked those big green eyes at him. "You hate grocery shopping?" she said slowly, as if it was Greek. "But…what do you cook?"

Her pained expression was absolutely adorable—and he was in pain again.

Josh shifted his hips, trying to ease his discomfort. "I don't," he declared through gritted teeth. "Oh, I nuke things in the microwave sometimes, but I haven't had a home-cooked meal in years."

"Oh, you poor thing!" Dani sank back into the rocking chair.

Now it was his turn to blink. A lack of hand-whipped potatoes and brown gravy earned him sympathy but not a drop of righteous indignation for what Carrie did? He started to fume again.

Then Michael burped. With dignity, of course. And Josh remembered exactly how much Dani valued children.

"If you're sure you want to watch Michael," she said as she rose from the chair and headed for the door, "I'll be glad to go shopping."

Stifling a triumphant grin, Josh said, "Just get breakfast

stuff. I've got a list of places that deliver. We can get Chinese, pizza—whatever you want.''

Dani turned in the doorway and gave him a smile that turned his insides to jelly. With the usual exception remaining rock-hard.

"Your take-out days are over, mister," she vowed. "As soon as you hand over the car keys. Oh, and I'll need directions," she added, then flushed. "And some money."

"No problem. Come on!" Josh loped downstairs, drew her a map, signed some blank checks, tossed her the keys and practically shoved her out the door.

"I checked my messages while you and Mom were bonding," he told Michael as they stood in the doorway and watched Dani chug away. "The Endicott case is heating up, which means I'll have to go into the office tomorrow. So let's play now—you can nap when Mom gets back."

Josh carried his baby back inside and discovered almost immediately that his earlier observation had been prophetically accurate: week-old infants weren't much fun. In fact, they couldn't play at all.

They could, however, cry. They could also squall. Sob. Wail.

Loudly. Relentlessly. Continuously.

An hour cried—er, crawled by. The longest hour of his life. At the end of which, Josh knew what the baby *didn't* want. Changing. Patting. Music. Rocking. Television. Reading aloud. Darkness. Light. Quiet. Noise. Being left alone for nearly twenty seconds. Being carried.

How on earth do people stand this day after day? Josh wondered, getting tenser by the teardrop as the baby cried against his shoulder. In his carrier. In the new crib. On a blanket on the living room floor. On Josh's bed. In the playpen.

In sheer desperation, he filled the Baby's First Bath with an inch or so of warm water—and Michael. The crying slowed, but didn't stop. Grimly, Josh ran water in the regulation tub and floated the baby bath in it. Better.

Just as he reached the frayed end of his rope, he finally stumbled on something that soothed his poor, frazzled baby.

Sound effects.

Arms loaded with grocery sacks, Dani let herself into Josh's town house. She'd put a sizable dent in his checkbook balance, but honestly— A quick survey before leaving had revealed that Josh's refrigerator held a bottle of catsup, one beer and an inky jar of salad peppers. The pantry contained only dust.

I'll put away the rest later, she decided after depositing the perishables in the refrigerator. Then, brushing wayward curls off her face, she went in search of—*Michael.*

And Josh. She even had an excuse. The sacker agreed with her that the station wagon he'd bought in No Lake was practically a classic that just needed a little TLC.

Reaching the foot of the staircase, she heard— *What the heck?* It sounded like a hand-held mixer with hiccups.

"Josh?" she called, climbing the stairs as fast as she could. "Michael? Where are you?"

As she took the last step and hurried into the nursery, Josh's deep voice came from the connecting bathroom, whose door was ajar. "We're in here."

Dani halted on the threshold. "Are you okay?" she asked.

"Fine. Peachy." There was a strange flat tone to his voice. "Come on in."

She hesitated, chewing on her lip. What if he was naked? Just getting out of the shower? Images of that taut, tanned, incredibly male body—in all its natural glory—flashed through her mind and sent those coils of heat through her like strokes of lightning.

Get over it.

How? snapped the part of her that wanted to be this man's woman.

The same way you got through the last six months. One day, one step at a time.

Taking a deep breath, Dani poked her head around the door.

And had to grab the door molding as her knees threatened to give way.

Even bedraggled, Josh was a magnificent specimen of male power and sensuality.

He knelt beside the tub, his T-shirt soaked and clinging to his hard, muscular form like an illicit second skin, his hair sticking up every which way, his jaw sculpted from granite....

Towels huddled in various corners of the room. Water spotted the floor, the mirror over the sink, the—

"Good gravy, Josh!" she exclaimed. "What happened?"

Before he could answer, the baby in the little blue bathtub whimpered. With a lopsided smile, Josh turned his attention back to her son and started making— *Motorboat noises.*

Michael yawned, tucked his fist under his ear and went to sleep.

"Finally." Josh sagged against the tub, then reached for one of the towels stacked on the commode lid. Lifting Michael out of his bathtub, he carefully wrapped the baby in the thick terry cloth. "Here." He handed son to mother.

Without saying another word, Josh stood, dried his arms and wrinkled-prune hands on a fresh towel, then dropped it on the floor. Dani had a feeling he didn't even realize it had left his fingers. "I'll, uh...I'd better..." he mumbled to the far corner of the tub enclosure as he stepped over the used towel and eased past mother and son. "Then I—"

"Josh. What happened?"

He ran a hand through his dampened hair and gave a ragged sigh. At last, he looked at her, and the raw anguish in his turquoise eyes sliced right through her.

Instinctively she stretched a hand to him, but though his skin was warm, his eyes turned cool and distant, his jaw went titanium and his long fingers curled into fists against his thighs.

"Don't worry. Michael's okay. Not great, but..." Then the toneless barricade faltered and there was a desperate edge to his voice that tore her heart out. "I'm so sorry, Dani! The poor kid wanted—*needed*—something, but...I couldn't figure out what—he had to cry and cry. I swear to you, I didn't mean to make him so unhappy."

Dani glanced down at her sleeping son. "Yeah, he really looks upset, doesn't he?" she said with a smile. "He's only a week old," she gently reminded the Viking warrior who'd been vanquished by an infant. "This is all as new to him as it is to us. Sometimes I think *he* doesn't know what he wants."

"I never realized how hard it is to be a baby," Josh said in a soft, broken voice, touching Michael's cheek tenderly with one finger before he backed away. "But I... Maybe that's why Carrie..." His voice faded, then he shook his head regretfully. "I'm sorry, Dani. I guess I'm not cut out for this."

She kept her hands clasped around the baby. Because she wanted—more than she'd ever wanted anything in all her twenty-three years—to reach for Josh, to ease his pain in the most elemental way. And to assure him that the only failure was refusing to try.

"I'll be downstairs," Josh said tonelessly, and disappeared.

After placing Michael in the crib, Dani subdued the bathroom, unpacked, and headed for the kitchen.

While she prepared a simple meal of oven-fried chicken, mashed potatoes and steamed zucchini garnished with chopped tomato, she heard computer sounds, a telephone, and Josh's deep voice coming from the living room.

Her fears that dinner might be awkward proved groundless: thanks to Michael, they ate in shifts.

In fact, their only direct contact the remainder of that day came as the midnight feeding concluded. A slight noise alerting her, Dani turned to see his huge, male shape outlined by the faint light filtering through the window.

"Josh..." As she breathed his name, he plucked Michael from her arms and in one motion, covered his shoulder with a pad and settled the baby against it.

"Dinner was delicious, but you must be exhausted. Go to bed, Dani. I'll burp him." The words were so soft and deep, they seemed to form inside her head like clouds.

When she started to speak, he laid a callused finger against her lips. "No," he said. "Just go. He's almost asleep so... I won't screw this up," he promised.

What could she say that wouldn't betray her foolish heart? With a helpless sigh, she went.

The next morning she had breakfast ready when Josh came downstairs clad in a custom-tailored charcoal suit that adored his bold, masculine beauty. He also wore a blindingly white shirt, an understated silk tie—and an aloof, preoccupied expression.

Her sweet, handsome slob, magically transformed into a sophisticated, successful attorney, hid behind the sports section while he devoured perfectly scrambled eggs and melt-in-your-mouth biscuits.

Finished, Josh let the paper slide to the floor as he stood and thanked the top of the refrigerator for breakfast, then asked if it needed anything. When Dani shook her head and that braid shimmered, he got the hell out of there before he grabbed it, reeled her in and took her right there on the kitchen table. "Don't hold up dinner," he said over his shoulder. "I'll be late."

He'd made the decision last night. Between Dani's ever-stronger appeal and his failure with Michael, Josh had no safe choice but retreat.

By sheer willpower, he managed to immerse himself in work all day every day that week, staying too busy to wish for another second chance.

Until Saturday.

Chapter Six

"**W**hat are you doing here?" Josh asked, surprised to see Marletta at her desk, wielding a red pencil, when he let himself into the office on Saturday morning.

The secretary snorted. "I'm trying to get some work done." Her red pencil kept moving. "What's your excuse?"

I'm avoiding temptation. "I work here, too—remember?"

"Humph. You haven't spent five minutes bein' productive this whole week. Why start now?"

"That's not true."

Damn the woman! There was enough ice in his voice to sink a transatlantic liner; she just sailed right past it.

"Oo-oh. I stand corrected," Marletta said with her patented laconic sarcasm. "Let's see... In the past five days, you returned three or four phone calls. Wrote a letter..."

Josh's secretary jabbed her red pencil in his direction. "Mostly you sat in your office all week, keepin' an eye on the furniture."

"I was catching up on my reading," he declared. Well, it was worth a shot.

"Uh-huh." The two syllables were loaded with more skepticism than a White House reporter.

And her suspicions were valid, of course. He'd held law journals open in front of him for hours on end. Occasionally remembered to turn a page, but he hadn't read a single article.

How could he? He kept hearing Michael cry.

With a groan, Josh sank onto the leather love seat provided for waiting clients and buried his head in his hands. All those years he'd held that grudge against Carrie for denying him a chance at fatherhood—and he was no good at it.

"Walker. Hey, Walker, snap out of it." Marletta sounded genuinely concerned.

No wonder Carrie hadn't consulted him. No wonder Dani's pine green eyes held shadows when she looked at him. Intimately acquainted with him in one way or another, they *knew*...

Marletta's normally fluid tones sharpened. "Hey, bag the misery, will ya?

"You're the boss, remember? If you want to goof off once in a while, go ahead. In fact," she continued in a suddenly bland tone that put Josh on red alert, "why don't you take next week off? You know, stay home with your...guests."

"No!" Lord knew, he *wanted* to. He missed Michael.

Every night he'd go home late, eat something delicious Dani had left in the oven, vow to go straight to his own room—and end up slowly pacing the nursery floor, carefully rubbing the baby's back until he expelled those pesky milk bubbles and fell asleep. Then he'd stand silently beside the crib, absorbing every little sigh and gurgle and the adorable, scrinched-up faces Michael made while he slept...

Michael's mama makes faces in her sleep, too, Josh thought with a smile, then frowned. He felt like a damned voyeur checking on her while she slept, but...he worried about her overdoing it. There was evidence of it everywhere: the living room almost eerily tidy, clothes he'd forgotten he owned were appearing, clean and pressed, in his closet and dresser, and those delicious smells filling the house—pot roast, lasagna, that heavenly chocolate meringue pie last night....

He just had to tiptoe into Dani's room after leaving Michael! Had to straighten the covers and tuck them around her. Had to smooth back the tendrils of hair escaping her braid and whisper his thanks for everything.

Didn't have to bend down and brush her soft cheek with his lips, though.

That was the other reason he didn't dare hang at the house. At the office, he could almost convince himself Dani Caldwell was just another woman, but the minute he heard her sweet, slow drawl or the silly nonsense she crooned to Michael, or saw her eyes sparkling like dew-soaked summer grass, or her lips curved in one of her mischievous smiles...he wanted to kiss her again, hold her, take her upstairs to—

"No!" he repeated. He thought he understood a little better what she meant about forgiveness, now that he'd faced his own terrible flaws, but Dani deserved more than he could give. So the fewer entanglements between them, the better. She and Michael would be gone soon and then...

Then he'd experience *real* loneliness. Josh sighed.

"Okay!" Marletta threw the red pencil down on her desk, then snatched it up again. "Okay. Sit in there and mope till you turn to stone," she said slowly, taking the red cylinder in both hands. "But, if you don't come clean about what's really goin' on, mister, my retirement starts today."

"Oh, come on, Marletta, nothing's—"

The red pencil snapped in two. Josh stared at her, then groaned. He'd forgotten that hair trigger on her temper.

She brandished a pencil stub like a saber. "Don't you spread any more of that bull manure, sonny. Ever since I've known you, Walker, you've done nothing but work. Even your so-called vacations, you go out to Montana and help your brother punch cattle. You've got—'' Marletta started ticking items off fingers ''—no hobbies, no friends, no love life. Nothing.

"Then one day, out of the blue, I get a call. 'Fix up a nursery for me. I'm bringing home a baby.' And then what?"

Marletta tossed the pencil parts at the trash can as she answered her own question. "Then nothin'. No explanation. No descriptions. Not even a picture of this supposedly incredible infant. You just waltz back into the office like nothin' happened." She was practically shouting now.

Abruptly, she lowered the volume and her voice resonated with sympathy. "Only…something *did* happen, and I want to know what it was."

He tried denial, but she rejected it before he got past *N* to head for *o*.

"Look. From the first day you hired me, I never pried, did I? Even though any fool could see that something or somebody was eatin' you up inside. But this time a baby's involved and you're so upset you can't stuff it away, can't get a lick of work done. So spill, Walker, or I'm outta here."

Josh turned. Intending to stalk regally into his office and slam the door. If she wanted to quit, let her. He wasn't baring his soul again. Not even to Marletta.

And yet, after one step, he came to a halt. Because words began pouring out of him like coins from a slot machine.

He heard himself tell her about the flash flood and Dani going into labor. Then backtrack to cover law school and Carrie's betrayal. Finally, Josh described his disastrous experience with Michael, sparing no detail of his own pathetic failure.

"So you see," he finished, wondering ironically why taking Annie's advice to quit feeling sorry for himself seemed to involve so much talking about the very subject he'd avoided like the damned plague all these years. For some weird reason, though, "picking at the scab" didn't hurt as badly this time; he wasn't as raw underneath it. "I've spent all this time outraged and sick with wanting something I shouldn't have—because I'm lousy at it."

"Let me get this straight," Marletta said, her mouth twitching as she picked up a new pencil and stuck it in her hair. "You've been hiding in this office all week be-cause...because a baby cried at you?"

Josh frowned at his secretary. Michael most certainly was not just any baby. He was— *Dani's baby. Not mine, even if I still wish he could be.*

"I'm not hiding," he protested automatically. "But didn't you hear me? I tried everything I could think of and I couldn't calm him down. He cried for almost an hour."

Marletta's laughter rolled through the room like a river in spring flood. "Walker, you slay me," she said when the flow dropped to the occasional chuckle. "Listen here, my Lorene once cried for a week solid.

"Do you know how to ride a bike?" she asked, changing the subject abruptly.

"What does—"

"Just answer the question," Marletta commanded.

He should have never let her near those books on cross-examination techniques.

"You can't equate bicycles and babies, Marletta. Bike riding's a learned skill. Parenting is an instinct. You either have it or you don't."

Josh thrust resigned fingers through his hair. "And I don't." He could hear the bleakness in his voice and didn't care. He was tired of hiding his feelings. "I had no idea what Michael wanted, how to make him happy.

"What a doofus I am," Josh said in disgust, shaking his head as he shoved his hands to the bottom of his pockets. "All that garbage I used to tell myself about the injustice of being denied my chance at fatherhood...and all along—"

"Oh, can it, Walker," Marletta interrupted.

Darn woman didn't even respect devastation.

"Having five children makes me the rug rat expert around here. And I'm telling you, instinct just makes you want to care for the child. It sure doesn't tell you how, 'cuz each child, each stage, is different. What works with one may bomb with another."

She shook a schoolmasterly finger at him. "You learn parenting by doing it. So why don't you go home and get in a few lessons with that baby you're crazy about?

"And with his mama," Marletta added, flashing her smarmiest, know-it-all smile. "You're crazy 'bout her, too, aren't you?"

Josh felt his face grow hot. "I don't—"

Even if he wanted to, he didn't dare risk his heart on Dani Caldwell. A man only got one second chance, after all—and she'd seen him at his worst. Several times. She'd reject him in a heartbeat. Besides... "She's a widow," he protested.

"That means her husband's dead," Marletta observed. "Not her. Of course, she'd have to be pretty desperate to get involved with someone like you...." She paused to study Josh's face, long enough to make him uncomfortable, wondering what she saw there that made her own expression grow so solemn.

As usual, she didn't keep him in suspense for long. "Aw, shoot, Walker, you're somethin' of an idiot on occasion. But basically, you're a good person. You deserve some happiness. If Dani's what you want, go for it."

Josh rubbed a hand over his jaw. Damn, he'd smelled those waffles this morning and forgotten to shave again. Rushed downstairs just as Dani lifted one out of the waffle iron and plated it. She'd made some kind of raspberry syrup from scratch, too. Lordy, those things tasted like ambrosia!

"And if she's what you *need*," his secretary said, interrupting Josh's fond reminiscence, "don't let anything stand in your way."

Well, he didn't *need* anyone, of course, but...making love to Dani for the next forty or fifty years and raising Michael to manhood had a heck of a lot more appeal than scrambling around to find a woman who left him cold because she didn't have pine-forest green eyes, then exchanging security for a family.

"Love is somethin' you learn by doing, too," Marletta added.

With a grin, she waved the new pencil at him like a scepter. "So, just get the heck out of here, okay? Go home. I can't get any work done with you skulkin' around here."

Desire pounded through his veins. A little anxiety, too. No, that was *terror* racing through him. What if he proposed marriage—strictly a platonic one of convenience, of course—and Dani reacted so negatively she advanced her departure date?

What if he gave parenting another try and really couldn't master it? Would he have to hunt up Carrie and beg *her* forgiveness?

Or was that what Dani meant?

And what if he could *learn?*

Maybe he should give himself a second chance, too.

He wasn't ready to call his sister-in-law and tell her hell just froze over, but... Okay, maybe he *would* go home. Give himself another try with Michael. Sound out Dani's receptivity to a...merger. If the signals were positive, he just might have a hope of finally getting the future he'd given up on for six stubborn years.

Could he possibly have a child, a family of his own? *Could he have Dani?* His heart thundered in his chest. His jeans strangled him again.

"Dammit, Marletta," he said, matching her grin. "You're right. I *am* the boss. I'm going home." To give his second chance a real chance.

Unfortunately, the phone rang before he made it to the office door.

Foolishly, Josh took the call, then went home, but not to stay. To pack.

Dani and Michael weren't there.

A note on the kitchen table indicated they'd gone to the park across from the town homes' entrance.

For a moment Josh wanted to rush over there after them and blurt— *What?*

Nothing. Not yet, anyway.

But, dammit, he should be the one taking Michael to the park! To the zoo. To Little League and soccer practice. To Cub Scout meetings. A boy needs a father.

As much as I need Michael.

Huh. Let's see you sell that one to Dani, who knows how well you parented her son. And who deserves a man who could love her completely, permanently. Ready to try that?

Josh grabbed clothes and toiletries, scribbled a brief note at the bottom of Dani's and went to Cleveland instead.

Dani took a deep breath. After all she'd weathered— Jimmy's emotional desertion and drinking sprees, his death, her in-laws' threats to take Michael—she would not blubber over Josh leaving town for a week.

She'd do what she'd always done. While Josh Walker made himself scarcer than a summer snowstorm in Texas, she'd stay busy.

Room and board—that was the deal, she reminded herself as she settled Michael on his stomach in the playpen, gave the soup another stir and set up the ironing board. While Michael worked on holding his head up, she'd iron a few more of the shirts she kept finding in various corners of the house.

Dani filled the iron's water tank, flipped the tab to steam and set the temperature slide at cotton. *You're playing Cinderella,* she chided herself. *Living out your childhood dream*

*of a baby, a home, and a wonderful man…trying to forget
that midnight's approaching.*

Even if he did look and act the part, she reminded herself
sternly, Josh was only an absent stranger, not Prince Charm-
ing. And his masterful kisses were just…*impulses, not
promises.*

*Get practical. Come up with a career possibility that pro-
vides financial security* and *allows you time to be Michael's
mother.*

The baby squirmed mightily—and lifted his head off the
playpen pad for almost two seconds.

Dani grabbed a shirt and the spray starch, wishing Josh
was here to share the thrill of Michael's accomplishment.
But he wasn't.

A rueful smile escaped her. The man who stood up to
Bubba without flinching had been routed by an infant's
tears.

And by her meddling into his past.

Dani spread the shirt collar on the ironing board. With
almost two lonely weeks to think about it, she'd come to
the conclusion that she owed Josh Walker an apology. If he
wanted to be resentful and unforgiving, that was his right.
The only person he was hurting, after all, was himself.

She, on the other hand, would be endangering not only
herself, but an innocent child if she lost her heart to Josh
Walker.

She had trouble remembering that when he was around.
Shoot, when Josh was around, she had trouble remembering
anything—except that she was a woman, with a woman's
desires and needs.

And a baby who needed his mother's full attention.

The collar finished, Dani starched and steamed the yoke,
which reminded her of Josh's broad shoulders. From there—
flip the shirt, press a sleeve—she was right back to fanta-
sizing about his hot turquoise eyes, his sexy, lopsided smile.
Shoot, she even found his gruff exterior, one of those sim-

plistic male defense mechanisms designed to hide a heart of mush, endearing.

With a sigh, Dani ironed the second sleeve. She'd expected Jimmy to become a man like Josh. But Jimmy hadn't given himself—or her or his son—the chance.

Thinking about Michael and Josh had Dani wondering again if, for her baby's sake, she should consider marrying a second time.

She sprayed starch on the body of the shirt. Maybe she would—if she could just stop picturing this future partner with honey-gold hair and turquoise eyes...

Needing a legitimate reason for the sudden heat flooding through her, Dani hit the burst-of-steam button.

As she finished the first shirt and returned it to its hanger, she looked over at Michael, who'd worn himself out with head-lifts and leg-kicks and fallen asleep. Would her son be terribly disadvantaged growing up without a father? Without grandparents?

Indecision rocked her again. By refusing to even try to work out a compromise with the Caldwells, was she being as irresponsible and selfish as Josh's girlfriend had been? Had her decision to flee Texas left Michael's grandparents as bereft as Josh was?

But I can't give up Michael! He's all I have.

He's all Pete and Edna Caldwell have, too.

Dani reached for another shirt as she wrestled with her dilemma. She'd do a couple more, then Michael would be awake again and hungry. *After which, I'll quit this squirrelcage thinking and experiment with salad dressings,* she decided.

Let's see... She'd purée some garlic, add balsamic vinegar and olive oil. Whisk in a little mustard and honey, add some tarragon....

Maybe she could keep house and cook for a big, rambunctious family. Three or four kids and their parents, whose love for each other radiated through the family like

ripples spreading across a pond. Yeah, that might be perfect.
She and Michael would have an apartment over the garage
and—

Without references?

Dani positioned a gray, banded-collar shirt and applied
the iron firmly. If she had to sacrifice everything—home,
friends, romantic fantasies and Jimmy's grieving parents—
to keep her son, she would. Simple.

Still…when she got on her feet, she'd work on finding a
safe way to contact the Caldwells. She'd ask Josh how to
protect her legal rights first, though. If he ever returned from
Cleveland, where some toxic dumper picked the wrong old
lady's warnings to ignore.

That's what his note had said and his secretary confirmed.
Marletta called every day, asking if they needed anything,
dropping blatant hints about his abilities and successful
practice. Dani couldn't tell if the woman was bragging on
Josh or warning her off.

It didn't matter.

*In less than a month, Michael and I will just be memories
to Josh Walker, fading like old photos left in sunlight.*

Dani jerked the plug from the wall socket and wrapped
the cord around the iron. Enough of the pity party. Time to
create the world's greatest vinaigrette.

At Marletta's insistence, Josh called the office twice a
day. Since the docket date was approaching, Endicott's legal
team finally wanted to talk settlement.

He also dialed his home number a thousand times, but
never let it ring.

Well, it was either too late or too early or— What the
hell was he going to say over the phone?

He worked furiously on the new case, but still, he was
stuck in Cleveland through the weekend and for four more
interminable days. Dammit! Almost three of their six weeks
gone.

Evenings in Ohio dragged like a tractor in deep mud, so Josh found a bookstore and loaded up on child-rearing books. Studied them at night instead of surfing cable channels or organizing his legal notes. The paper experts agreed with Marletta: successful parenting involved trial and error. They, too, assured him that love and willingness offset nearly any mistake.

Love is something you learn by doing, too.

"But not in Cleveland," he muttered, glaring out the rain-spattered hotel window at a glowing blob of light across town: Jacobs Field, where some fools were trying to play baseball despite the weather. Josh kicked aside his shaving kit and stomped on yesterday's tie as he prowled the room restlessly. Baseball, bah.

Double bah for the idiot who picked a career path that required him to practice law all over the damned country-side.

He wanted to be home with his baby, dammit! And with the woman who could teach him...everything he'd refused to learn for so long. Then maybe someday he could have a baby of his own. A baby like Michael.

Why not the genuine article? Josh's heart pounded as he considered the possibility for the hundredth time. *Yeah, why not Michael himself?*

That would mean marrying Michael's mother.

For a second Josh contemplated it. Imagined Dani. In his life. In his bed, her hair tumbling down over his—

Not exactly a hardship.

Unless she expected what every wife deserves. To be loved and cherished.

He wondered if he was capable of loving a woman, even one as incredible as Dani. What he'd felt for Carrie had been fleeting, already waning when he'd learned about the tragic consequences of immaturity and self-indulgence. Of heedlessness.

Our heedlessness. "Carrie's mistake," he admitted to the frozen silence of six years. "And mine."

Drifting back to the window of his room, watching fat raindrops slide down the glass and slick the streets with silver moisture, Josh finally took Dani's advice. Set aside his rancor and faced his own part in the tragedy.

If Carrie had betrayed him, he'd failed her, too. By not being responsible. Not being supportive. Not communicating enough to save his now-lost-forever child.

Josh slid his hands into his pockets as a car drove past the hotel, its taillights painting red brushstrokes down the wet street. Leaning his forehead against the cool glass, he closed his eyes and felt the last hard knot of grief and resentment dissolve inside his chest.

Once again, Dani's words echoed in Josh's head. *It's not about forgiveness.*

He still wasn't sure he understood, but he could move forward now, instead of twisting his gut around the past in a futile effort to transform it.

With a sigh of release, he turned to start packing. Smiled a little as he dredged shoes and underwear and a cuff link out from under the bed and stuffed it all into his overnight bag. Disassembled his laptop and encased it. Piled his bags by the door and took a flying leap across the room to land spread-eagled on the bed.

Flopping over on his back, Josh grinned at the ceiling blobs.

He'd have to revisit Cleveland soon, but in the morning, he was going home. To tell Dani he understood how fruitless his years of icy anger had been. To ask for another shot with Michael. Take a few lessons in living. Make some amends.

And if the lady was willing—

No, Josh thought with a stab of regret. Dani's had one flawed husband already. He couldn't ask her to take on another bozo whose heart, no matter how healed, remains scarred.

That still left three weeks with his baby. And if Dani decided she needed more time to recuperate...*I'm always willing to negotiate. Especially with a green-eyed Texas angel.* Josh grinned at the blobs again. *Or two.*

Leaping up, he searched the room for a pillow. Retrieved one from behind the TV and fell asleep—smiling—the instant his head hit the waxy hotel pillowcase.

Dani heard the front door a second before she closed the washer lid. Resisting temptation, she twisted the dial to the proper cycle setting and started the load of laundry before she ineffectively smoothed a hand over her unruly hair, took a deep breath and headed toward the foyer.

He was standing at the entrance to the living room, luggage and a huge teddy bear clasped in one hand, his blond hair gleaming above the black trench coat covering his broad shoulders.

Her knees threatened to buckle. She wanted to call his name, then launch herself into his arms when he turned. *Oh, grow up,* she told herself. *Life's not a movie and you're not his leading lady.*

Even if you want to be.

She must have made some sound because he turned around and her heart slammed against her ribs, ignoring her head's warnings. Every feminine part of her ached for this man, for his touch, his smile, his mouth on hers.

"Hi, Dani." Wariness lurked in his turquoise eyes. Well, that was an improvement over the bleak anguish she'd seen the day they'd arrived and she'd abandoned him to the mysteries of infancy. "It's...it's nice to have something to come home to," he said, his voice deep and velvety.

Silly heart leaped again, then crashed back to earth as he continued, "What's that wonderful smell?"

"Apple cake." She pushed the words past dejected tonsils.

Josh turned back to study the living room. "Well, uh, how are you, Dani? How's Michael?"

"I'm fine. He's sleeping.

"Thanks to that great invention, the pacifier," Dani added with a smile.

He whirled, but she was the one who got dizzy. "The *what?*" Josh demanded.

"Michael kept fussing," she explained. "So, finally, I called a local pediatrician. Her nurse said some babies just need to do more sucking than others."

"You mean it—" His turquoise eyes heated up and that irresistible lopsided smile slowly appeared. "It really wasn't me?"

Oh, the poor, darling man. Dani blinked back tears as she tried to recall one time Jimmy had accepted responsibility for the problems he'd caused—and here was Josh taking the blame for a baby's natural behavior.

"No, Josh," she assured him. "It wasn't you."

After a long moment he nodded and deposited his luggage beside the bear. He turned toward the living room again and cleared his throat.

"What did you mean," he asked abruptly, "when you said it's not about forgiveness?"

Dani clasped her hands in front of her nearly flat stomach and uttered a silent prayer for the right words. "Forgiveness implies the right to judge others. That's not our job."

Turning again to face her, Josh looked confused, but there was something...*open* about him for the first time since they'd met through his broken windshield.

So Dani used her own pain to explain. "Look, my parents thought I hung the moon. But Jimmy's dad was always measuring him. Always expecting more than he could give. I simply *can't* know how that affected Jimmy. So how do I judge his behavior if I can't really understand his pain?

"I don't. The only person I'm qualified to judge is myself."

Josh growled, then raked fingers through his hair. "Then, is there... Are you saying that my loss, all the suffering—mine *and* Carrie's—was all for nothing?"

Dani shook her head. "We can't change the past, but we can pay it honor and give it meaning by not forgetting the lessons it teaches us."

He looked at her so long she thought she was going to start squirming like a kid caught unprepared in class. "For someone so young," Josh said finally in his deep, dark voice, "you have a lot of wisdom to offer. Once again, I think I owe you my life. Thank you," he added softly.

Then he took a step forward and kissed her. Lightly. Gently.

And Dani's heart turned over. Despite her hard-won knowledge and endless warnings, she was clearly teetering on the verge of falling in love with Josh Walker.

Or maybe I'm already there.

"You've, ah, been busy, I see," Josh said to break the awkward silence. "The place looks...I don't know, different."

"I picked up a little, that's all."

"Ha. You probably needed a shovel," Josh said, flashing his lopsided grin that heated the coils of desire inside her. "But it's more than that."

He cocked his head to one side as he pivoted on one foot to survey the living area again. "I can't put my finger on what you did, but the room's...well, inviting now."

"I, uh, rearranged the furniture a little." She suspected the delivery crew had created the boring placement she'd altered. "Do you mind?"

Josh didn't answer, just ambled into and around the room.

"I..." She swallowed her regret. *His house, his life, his furniture. None of my business,* she reminded herself fiercely. "I can move it all back to its origi—"

He held up a hand to stop her. "No, it's great! It's just…"

Quick, you idiot—think! He wanted an extension of their agreement and for that, he needed a plan. Some way to make Dani feel invested here. In Virginia. In his house. In him.

"I've got some vacation scheduled and…" Josh glanced wildly around again. With the furniture redistributed and the layers of sporting equipment and cast-off clothes removed, the living room looked— Ha! He waved his hand at the room. "I, uh, planned to do something about all that beige."

Dani goggled those forest-glade eyes at him. "You mean, paint the walls?"

Not alone, dammit. "Don't you think a little color would help the place?"

"Well…" She tugged on her lower lip as she gazed at the bland Sheetrock. "What color were you thinking of?"

"I was hoping you'd have some suggestions." His were probably still illegal in the state of Virginia, as well as physically impossible for— "Aren't you and Michael due for checkups soon?" he asked, then went on before she could answer. "We'll do that this week, too."

"Anything else, master?" Dani asked with her mischievous grin, making him instantly hard again.

A hundred erotic suggestions came immediately to mind. After a slow inhalation to ensure he could control himself, Josh nodded. "Yeah," he said, flashing a grin of his own. "How about a piece of that apple cake?"

"Coming up," Dani said, and led the way to the kitchen.

There was a disassembled something-or-other from the old clunker on the counter next to the cake. "I'm rebuilding a few of the engine parts," Dani replied to his question about it as she cut him a slice of cake.

"Lord, woman," Josh asked after his first taste of the moist, flavorful dessert. "Is there anything you can't do?" *Except love me, that is.*

He'd never expect that—no matter how much he was beginning to suspect he wanted it. Even Texas angels had their limits.

Chapter Seven

They painted the living room orange. Well, Dani called it persimmon or melon or something. He had to admit it looked pretty good, especially after they refreshed the trim, too.

Not as good as Dani in a pair of skintight jeans....

Josh managed to keep rolling cantaloupe-colored paint over the bland beige wall while his mind floated off to its favorite image. Him making love to Dani.

Or better yet, vice versa.

Desire streaked through him, hot and demanding.

She leaned over to paint the last foot of baseboard on an adjacent wall.

"Dammit, Dani!" he roared as his jeans threatened to strangle his, er, excitement. "I mean, bend at the knees before you strain your back."

His outburst surprised her into looking up from her work. A tactical error if she aimed to keep her heart in line until he went back to the office.

Look at him. Wearing more paint than the wall, hadn't

shaved this morning and he still had enough sex appeal for six or seven movie stars.

He also expected sarcasm. She could see it in the set of his jaw. So she twinkled her eyes at him, folded her legs to sit on the floor, then asked sweetly, "Did you study chiropractic medicine before or after law school?"

"During," he retorted, grimacing as the loaded roller dripped orange latex in his ear. "Same time I saved the whales, provided free debt counseling and taught Sunday school."

Dani's lips twitched. And so, unless she was mistaken, did Josh's. "You must be eligible for sainthood, then."

"Not till Tuesday," he snapped.

And suddenly they were laughing. Then Josh tilted his head to let the paint run out of his ear, dropped the roller, stepped on it, lost his balance and wound up with one hand completely immersed in the roller tray. They laughed some more.

In fact, they spent most of the day laughing.

Living out Dani's dream.

It wasn't a very big dream. Just a house turned into a home, two or three babies to love, someone with whom to share the ups and downs of life. Dani sighed. She grew more afraid every day that her special someone had turquoise eyes, a gruff disguise for his tender heart, and the lithe, tawny grace of a mountain lion.

Josh had to death squeeze the paint rag against his orange fingers to keep from reaching for her. He wanted to tease away Dani's sigh with slow strokes along her satiny skin, to comb his fingers through her hair, then take her mouth with his. Wanted to give her...

What? And would it be enough? Would I be enough?

Tearing his gaze from her sexy, denim-clad legs, Josh took slow, deep breaths until he could say blandly, "Well, now that we've set the walls on fire—" *and my libido, too, as usual* ''—don't you think the rest of the room looks sort of lame?''

So while he cleaned pumpkin-colored drips from the windows and Michael slept off lunch, Dani went into Fallsboro. Brought back rectangles of fabric and pieces of foam—and a timing light and a set of spark plugs, announcing she intended to tune the clunker's engine.

''Great,'' Josh agreed. As long as he could sit with Michael and chat while she worked.

Later that afternoon, after Michael's high tea feeding, she wrapped the foam in the fabric, knotted here and folded there and—ba-boom!—big, bold pillows lounged on his sofa.

The room instantly looked warmer, more appealing than it ever had.

Huh? Well, Josh wasn't a complete idiot. Shown the difference between a house and a home, he could see it. Just as he'd learned to appreciate clean clothes—hanging where they could be easily located—and home-cooked meals featuring real food. He knew who was responsible for it all, too.

And who wasn't.

Clearly, he needed a woman with more than fertility going for her. He needed someone like Dani who understood the mysteries that eluded him, things like ambience and baby moods, aesthetics and emotion.

Why hadn't he ever realized there was more to life than work? More to raising a child than providing financial support and playing games with him?

He should have. *He* should have. After his mother's death, his dad continued to love him and his brothers, of course. Worked from sunup to sundown to feed, clothe and educate them. But the flavor, the richness of life, had died with his mother.

Any baby of his was going to have a loving home. And

that could only happen, Josh realized, if he and the baby's mother loved each other.

For a second, cold panic gripped Josh's heart as he scraped paint off the windows while Dani fiddled in the garage. She couldn't possibly love him. What was to love? Hell, every time he tried to help her, *she* dragged *his* tail to safety.

As he pushed the blade back and forth over the glass, Josh replayed the kisses they'd shared.

Okay, maybe she wasn't completely indifferent to him. But exactly how interested was she?

Hmm. He didn't dare make any blatant moves without some active encouragement, of course, but if he could manage to fit a little careful research into his investment plan....

So the following day, he dragged her—and Michael, of course—off to Alexandria to tour art galleries, poke through antique stores and graciously accept "darling baby" comments on Michael's behalf.

And he *was* darling. Undoubtedly, the most adorable infant ever born.

Every day, Michael taught Josh a new appreciation for the beauty and complexity of ordinary life.

And made him want—more and more, if that was possible—to help a baby grow up.

This baby. He wanted to stick with the kid—and the woman—who'd brought him this far. If they'd stay. The six weeks of their agreement were vanishing like smoke in a windstorm.

Well, hell, Walker. You make your living being persuasive. Get to work.

The morning after they bought a painting to hang above the fireplace and a few little knickknack things in the antique stores, Josh announced that he'd been meaning to landscape his postage-stamp backyard but... Turning his palms up, he shrugged as helplessly as he knew how. "I don't know a thing about plants,'' he said, trying to gaze puppylike into her forest-glade eyes.

Luckily, instead of laughing, Dani bought it.

Which earned him a trip to the gardening place, then home to dig holes and mix dirt and sand and— Josh thought he'd better inform his brother that his livestock was leaving a fortune in fertilizer in his pastures.

By dinnertime—the best meat loaf, mashed potatoes and corn on the cob he'd ever tasted—he'd worked up a good sweat and Dani had turned the little strip of grass surrounding his patio into a bright, attractive border of flowers and foliage.

In one area, though, his plan failed completely. Citing Dr. Ravjani, Josh tried to declare afternoons as rest time. Perfect for personal bonding.

Dani refused to cooperate. If she wasn't at Michael's beck and call, she was cooking, cleaning, or tinkering with that old clunker. The only way he found to slow her down was to insist she sit down and give him ''a potential juror's'' feedback on the Cleveland case.

Good thing he did—she pointed out a huge hole in his argument.

Thursday, after getting Marletta started on filling the hole, he caught Dani sneaking out of the house with some story about needing a part for the damned car.

"You're not going anywhere, sweetheart!" he roared, fearful her escape attempt was evidence of his plan's failure. "You promised you'd rest this afternoon. I knew I should sell that thing for scrap," he grumbled.

"Sc-rap?"

Lordy, when Dani's green eyes sparkled like that, he had to stuff his hands in his back pockets to keep from reaching for her.

But he *had* learned something useful from his experience with Carrie.

This time, nobody was getting hurt by premature consummation. If it killed him, he wasn't kissing her, caressing her, making love with her until they'd thoroughly discussed a more permanent relationship.

There was, however, nothing illegal about imagining intimacy with Dani. Thinking of her slim feminine form, naked, above him, while his hands, his mouth, his body brought her to passion's peak. And took them both over....

"Do you know how great it could be?"

Huh? Oh... "The car, you mean?" Josh grinned.

"All it needs is some paint and a brake job. That's why I wanted to check the salvage yard for brake drums."

Josh let her words flow past him.

Okay. If necessary, he'd try Plan B: find a compatible woman, exchange financial security for a family. But he'd much rather go with Plan A: make love to Dani for the next forty or fifty years and raise Michael as his own.

"Well, could you?"

"Could I what?" Josh frowned. Be a good father? He'd try like hell, was willing to take classes, but...

"Go to the salvage yard and make sure they pull the right drums while I rest?"

Bah, when she chewed on her lip like that, he'd sprout wings and fly around the Washington Monument if she asked him to.

"I wouldn't know a brake drum from a kettledrum," he confessed cheerfully. A good plan must be flexible.

So, with a blinding smile, Josh said, "Let's go together."

Dani blinked. The man was lethally loaded with charm.

And she was vulnerable to it. To him. Every minute she spent with Josh Walker was dangerous. This week had been the most delicious torture she'd ever endured. They'd joked and laughed and worked and talked and cared for Michael. Together.

Sometimes he'd even look at her with a certain male heat in his summer-sky eyes, making her feel more womanly, more desirable than she'd thought possible.

"Well?" he asked, his legs braced apart, the whole Viking warrior image somehow enhanced by the baby in his arms. "Neither one of us knows a damned thing about cars," Josh added, hitching Michael higher on his hip and making a silly face for the baby's benefit, "but we're willing to learn. Right, kiddo?"

Once again Dani yielded to the temptation to enjoy Josh's company while she could. She'd be on her own—and lonely soon. *Too darned soon.*

Nonsense. She'd stay busy giving Michael the loving home and unconditional approval Jimmy never had.

Single-handedly.

Because, face it, men like Josh Walker were as rare as Dallas debutantes who didn't like diamonds. And her heart—foolish heart—refused to settle for less.

Then you're on a collision course with heartache.

But she wouldn't need willpower to avoid that pain, she reminded herself. Time and distance would cure it for her. In just a couple of weeks she'd be telling Josh goodbye and taking Michael—somewhere. Probably back to Texas, where his grandparents would be close enough to visit.

"Okay," Dani said, tossing her braid over her shoulder. Until she left Josh's vicinity, there was no law against enjoying every conversation, cherishing every smile, savoring every kiss. "How soon can you be ready?"

Josh looked at his watch.

Dani looked at the crinkly hair covering his forearm. Which made her think about the dark cloud of same that dusted his massive chest and arrowed down his flat abdomen to foam around his—

Desire, as strong and hot as the Texas sun flooded through her.

Imagine his reaction if you suddenly crossed the room, cupped his hard jaw with both hands and planted a deep, lingering, passionate kiss on him.

The man would probably hurt himself laughing.

"It's almost time for Michael's next feeding," he said. "What say we visit Salvage Land after that?"

As if on cue, the baby emitted his "I'm hungry" cry. "Wow," Dani commented, lifting Michael from Josh's arms and heading for the stairs. "You sure know your babies, don't you?"

Josh's pleased expression kept her blood fizzing the whole time she nursed her son.

"I still say Michael smiled this afternoon," Josh said as the phone rang that evening. Since he was happily stuffed to the gills with gingered chicken, glazed carrots and homemade apple pie, his insistence was pretty laconic. Levering himself off the sofa, he added, "Just because the salvage guy has seven kids doesn't mean he knows anything."

Dani giggled as she shook her head, sending that braid shivering over her breast—and making Josh hard *again*. "Sorry, Michael's still too young. It was just gas."

Bah. Michael *had* smiled at their distorted reflections in the shiny wheelcovers while Dani crawled under that wreck to inspect—

As he curled his fingers around the receiver and lifted it to his ear, Josh growled, "He's advanced for his age. Even the doctor said so during his checkup.

"Walker," he told the phone absently. He ought to get one of those disposable cameras. Take some pictures before—

No. Think positive. There must be some way to build an airtight case for staying together for Michael's sake without stumbling into the emotional minefield known as love....

Marletta's rich contralto came through the line. "This is your lucky day, boy-o."

"It is?" Josh shook his head ruefully. True, both Dani and Michael had gotten checkups after buying brake drums. The doc had assured Josh that mother and son were doing fine.

That didn't mean she was going upstairs with him anytime soon. His big, lonely bed would stay that way a while longer. At least until he convinced Dani to settle for respect and admiration—*and me.*

"Timing is everything," Marletta informed him smugly. "I just called Elliston Perrodeaux's office and guess what? The senator's had a cancellation, so he'll meet you for dinner tomorrow."

"Tomorrow?" Josh groaned. A month ago the invitation would have thrilled him.

Now the summons just meant time away from Dani and Michael. Time he didn't have to lose. "I suppose I'd better see the old goat, then," he said with a sigh. "When and where?"

Marletta snorted. "Try to contain your enthusiasm, Walker. This *is* a superb opportunity. Dinner at the Commanders' Club tomorrow night—just you, the senator and..." Josh gritted his teeth when she paused for dramatic effect. "Your date."

"Oh, baby—Marletta, give yourself a raise!" The Commanders' Club was one of those exclusive establishments frequented by Washington movers and shakers. Josh had been there once and in his opinion, the place offered more snobbery from the waitstaff than decent food. But still, his heart thundered with hope. Maybe a taste of so-called glamorous Capitol life would impress Dani. Help her overlook his shortcomings. Forget the past. Agree to stay.

Plan B held no attraction; he wanted Plan A. Dani and Michael. "Double that raise if you can find a baby-sitter."

"Don't be ridiculous," Marletta retorted. "His Worship's aide said the senator will meet you in the bar at the Commanders' Club at eight, so I'll be over around seven, seven-fifteen, to meet the little tyke and listen to a million silly instructions from you and the new mom— You *are* taking Dani, aren't you?"

"If she'll go," Josh muttered before the implication of

the rest of his secretary's speech finally registered. "*You're* going to baby-sit?"

"I wouldn't miss this for the world," Marletta vowed with a chuckle. "I've got to meet the tag team that finally melted the ice around your heart."

Josh didn't waste any breath protesting his secretary's assumptions. "Deal. See ya at seven."

Hanging up, he went bounding upstairs, looking for Dani, who'd gone to bathe Michael. Nearly kissed her despite his honorable-celibacy intentions when she bought his yackety-yack about needing her company to save the nation's natural heritage for future whatsits.

Did kiss her when she asked him to baby-sit after Michael's morning feeding so she could shop for something appropriate to wear.

Once again, Josh saw those exploding galaxies, heard bells ringing.

Still reeling, he settled a towel-wrapped Michael in the crook of his arm and waved her off to work on the brakes or watch TV or whatever. While he lectured himself, probably unsuccessfully, on the virtue of patience.

When Dani came home the next day with a shopping bag and a smirk, Josh wanted her so much, he nearly suggested they can the senator and spend the evening upstairs. In his bed.

Idiot! As if one night with his Texas angel would be enough.

As if he'd risk losing his second chance for— Well, the guy at the salvage yard said seven kids were no more trouble than one.

For a moment Josh thought about Carrie's betrayal and the price they'd all paid as a result.

Out of that tragedy, he vowed, would come good. His lost child would always live in his memory, would help Josh be a better father.

To Dani's son. And maybe his own baby, too.

Josh hoped they'd have the same mother.

What if Dani turned him down? Married some other joker?

Red haze exploded around him.

So he called Endicott's lawyers and rattled their cage for a while. Then he hit the gym and practically tore a biceps lifting weights while he tried to convince himself that he wouldn't mind as long as the guy treated Dani and Michael okay.

Argued all the way home that, if necessary, he'd father a child with some other woman—who didn't have green eyes and maple-colored hair.

Argued without success.

That evening, Josh destroyed his bathroom, cut his chin shaving, and turned his bedroom into a landfill getting ready. He used a T-shirt to shine his shoes, dropped it beside a pile of discarded shirts and ties, slipped his wallet in his pocket and his watch over his wrist just as the doorbell rang.

Quickly, Josh glanced in the bathroom mirror. Let's see, hair combed, correct business dinner uniform: dark suit, white shirt, subdued tie. *Okay, Walker, you're as ready as you're gonna be.*

The doorbell sounded again. His heart started pounding. Tonight he'd exude all the charm, sophistication and erudition he possessed. Impress the hell out of his dinner partner.

He'd also try to be civil to the senator.

Striding to the bedroom door, he nearly tripped over a gym bag and a mound of sweaty workout clothes. *Damn, where did this stuff come from?*

The doorbell chimed one more time, then another.

"I'm coming," Josh shouted, shutting the door to his bedroom. He'd clean up that mess tomorrow. If anything, uh, unexpected occurred tonight, it could happen in Dani's bed. The first time.

Pausing outside her closed door, Josh sure as hell hoped this posh tête-à-tête with the senator would give him the edge he needed. That was really the only reason he'd accepted Perrodeaux's summons.

If it was up to Josh, they'd stay home, rent a video, watch Michael and go to bed early. Together.

Every night.

"Where's Michael?" he asked the wooden slab, barely throttling his urge to burst through that closed door and discover the exact nature of Dani's post-childbirth figure.

"Downstairs in his playpen," came the muffled reply. "I—I'm almost ready. I just—"

"Take your time," Josh said. "Marletta's a little early." And more than a little curious, no doubt.

He felt like a kid going to the prom, he mused as he cantered down the stairs and opened the front door to admit his secretary.

Then Josh ushered her into the living room so she could meet his baby. "Hey, tiger," he purred as he lifted Michael from the playpen. "Say hello to the bossiest woman you'll ever meet."

"Ahbaaa."

Josh beamed. "Isn't he the greatest?"

"Since sliced bread," Marletta agreed dryly, holding out her hands for the baby. "Come on, precious," she cooed, waggling her fingers.

"Bevooo," said Michael, and sort of lurched toward Josh's secretary.

Just as they completed the baby transfer, Josh heard a footstep on the foyer tile at the base of the stairs.

He spun around. Then just stood there gaping, like a Laplander seeing Miami for the first time.

Was this vision wearing a figure-hugging black dress with a short swirly skirt and tiny rhinestoned straps snaking over her bare, creamy-smooth shoulders his Dani Caldwell? Her legs went on forever. Her maple-colored hair had been subdued somehow, twisted into a knot atop her head.

His hands itched to find and remove whatever restrained it, then thrust themselves into the mass of curls as it tumbled over her—

"J-Josh?" Anxiety shadowed the green pools of her eyes; she was chewing on her lush lower lip. "Th-the saleslady said this would be appropriate...."

He made an odd sound, sort of a strangled groan.

"I'll just stay home with Michael, then," she said, lifting her chin to keep silly tears from falling. No sense in crying over spilled silk.

What a goose she was! Thinking a sophisticated Virginia lawyer would find her attractive. Thinking she could just trot along and have dinner with a United States senator. Her—a kid from Lufkin, Texas, whose education had been limited to learning how to face hard times and hard facts.

So, face 'em.

Keeping her head high, Dani forced out the words. "Y-you'd better go on. I'm sure Michael will be okay in his playpen while I change."

"Change?" Josh rasped. "Change what? Your mind?" His hand went to his tie, began wrenching the knot loose. "Fine. We'll stay home. I'd rather order pizza and have another piece of apple pie, anyway. Marlet—"

"Oh, Josh, stop it!" Dani snapped, then blinked in amazement as he froze obediently. "You can't stand up a senator."

"I most certainly will if you don't want to go."

Her heart lurched as she gazed at his suddenly granite jaw and recognized two more facts. Two earth-shattering facts.

Unlike her immature husband, Josh Walker meant what he said. He'd really risk his chance to influence Washington's power brokers just to keep her company if she refused to dine with Senator Perrodeaux.

And the power of dreams could not be denied. She loved Josh Walker. Maybe she had since she'd peered through his broken windshield. Love at first sight, again. But this time, this man—with his integrity, his stubbornness, his tenderness under the tough-guy image—deserved her love. Had earned her admiration and respect.

She also desperately wanted his lithe, powerful body. Wanted his gentle, rousing touches and his enchanting, melting kisses. And he'd already proven he was a great father.

Which made it simple. If she loved him—really loved him—she'd wish him happiness and let him go.

Josh needed a woman who'd be an asset to his career, who'd help him achieve the goals he'd set for himself.

The kid from Lufkin, the mother of somebody else's kid, isn't that woman, she told herself sharply. So, for Josh's sake and Michael's, she had to put a lid on her love. Otherwise her dreams and his would collide—leaving only two shattered adults and one bewildered innocent child.

"You're invited to stay, Marletta," Josh said as he unbuttoned his collar with a sigh.

No time like the present.

"I'm not dining with Senator Perrodeaux," Dani stated, narrowing her eyes. Ordinary people like her, and children like Michael, needed Josh's skill and any influence he could wield on their behalf. "But you are, mister. Just because I can't manage to dress properly is no reason for you to miss this opportunity."

"Dress properly?" Josh's turquoise eyes widened, then he half turned and flapped one hand at the attractive older woman gently jiggling a satisfied Michael. "Marletta. T-tell her."

"You look fine," the woman said between chuckles. "Really. I think the word is *stylin'*. That's why Walker's gone catatonic." Settling Michael securely in one arm, she grinned at Dani. "We've talked on the phone so much I feel I know you but, for the record, I'm Marletta Langtry."

"It's nice of you to volunteer tonight," Dani said, smiling at the steely determination in the other woman's chocolate eyes. "I see you've met my son." *And that you're not going to let me weasel out of this dinner disaster.*

"I'll take good care of your precious angel." The older woman smoothed her palm over Michael's fuzzy head with reassuring confidence. "You go have a little fun. In fact, there's a full moon tonight," Marletta added with an impish twinkle in her dark eyes. "Make Mr. Suave here show you the lights along the Potomac after dinner."

"Well...the phone num—" Dani started to say when Josh seemed to shake himself like a dog coming out of a lake.

"Right," he said, rebuttoning his collar and jerking his tie upward. "Have fun. Perfect dress. Phone number's on the refrigerator."

Pulling a thick sheaf of papers from his inside breast pocket, Josh shoved them at Marletta. "Here are a few notes on Michael's routine, habits, likes and dislikes. Dani left some formula in the fridge to supplement her, er, mother's milk."

After bending to kiss Michael's cheek, he took Dani's hand. "Come on, darlin'. Perrodeaux's a tiger about tardiness."

She went rigid, but he tugged her toward the door. "It's just dinner. And a little moonlight, uh, I mean, sight-seeing. Michael will be fine. Please, Dani?"

The man of her dreams called her *darlin'*. If she wasn't going to live in love ever again, couldn't she have one special night, one special memory of this magnificent male?

"Well..." Dani handed Josh the cropped jacket that matched the dress. "Promise you'll nudge me if I say something appalling."

Marletta snorted as she followed them to the door.

"Honey, he's not hearing anything but bells and rockets. You'll do fine."

Not bells and rockets. Rustling sheets. And soft, sexy little moans. As he drove this incredible woman over the edge and went sailing off to heaven with her.

She'd knocked him for a loop tonight. Again. Every time he thought he had her figured out—angel, mother, mechanic—she'd nonchalantly demonstrate some new talent, appear in some new guise.

"You're sure this dress is okay?" she asked a few minutes later as they drove through the Virginia countryside, cloaked in the blue haze of twilight.

"It looks fine."

Josh thought it would look even better sliding off her gorgeous body and hitting the floor while he wrapped her in his arms and took her down, down, down to the nearest mattress.

Where Dani, flushed with passion, would lean down and brush her long, silky hair over his—

"Really, Josh, I don't know what to say to a U.S. senator," she declared.

"The woman who handled Bubba before breakfast?" Josh laughed.

Twenty minutes later, he turned between two stone pillars bearing discreet bronze plaques. The old station wagon cruised majestically up the gently curving drive and floated to a halt under a white-columned porte cochere.

Josh dared the parking valet to snicker at their vehicle, but the kid just leaped forward to help Dani out.

"She's with me, sonny," he muttered, possessive red haze threatening again, and sprinted around the car to claim his...date.

Led her across thick Oriental rugs covering the acre of foyer, past flocked wallpaper and brooding French furniture. Down a paneled hallway until he heard generic piano music tinkling from a dark room on the right.

"In here, I imagine." He paused at the entrance. Dani peeked past his coat sleeve, catching a whiff of his pine scent.

The place pulsed quietly with money and power. Unfortunately, the men were merely second-rate imitations of Josh. The polished women wore diamonds and dresses very much like hers. *Only much more expensive.*

Dani smiled triumphantly—just as Josh leaned next to her ear and murmured, "That's him." He nodded toward a booth at the rear of the room. "Over there."

The man's white hair gleamed silvery in the room's subdued lighting. Heavily jowled and fingering a huge, unlit cigar, he exuded an aura of power that reminded Dani of Jimmy's father—times ten. She froze in her tracks.

Then Josh's strong hand touched her waist, his heat flowed over her chilled nerves.

She'd run once rather than challenge authority. Not this time. For Josh's sake, Dani led the way as they wove a path through the dimly lit ocean of tiny round tables.

"There you are, Walker," the senator boomed as they approached. "Right on time." The two men shook hands, then the senator half rose from his seat as Josh introduced Dani, who mumbled something polite.

"Sit down, sit down," Perrodeaux boomed again, the syllables dipped deep in Dixie and Southern-fried. He raised a pudgy hand and a waiter appeared. "Thought we'd have a drink here before we adjourn to the dining room."

Perrodeaux looked at Dani, who shook her head silently. The waiter waited. So did Josh. The bulky, white-haired senator preferred action. "Don't be shy, little lady," he barked loudly enough to turn heads. "Anythin' you want. Glass o' wine, one of those frosty drinks with an umbrella in it—"

"Uh, I'll have a club soda, please," Dani said finally.

"You one of those recoverin' alcoholics, missy?"

Dani was just about to quietly slide off the seat and disappear under the table when she glanced at Josh. The clown was grinning at her. With that lopsided smile that turned her insides to mush.

"Go on," he urged her. "Tell the senator why you're drinking club soda."

Her cheeks burned, but— "I'm, uh, still nursing my baby." Although tonight's introduction to infant formula was part of Dani's plan to begin weaning him from breast milk, a necessity if she was going to work.

And she'd been unable to come up with any other way to provide all those silly things children needed: food, clothing, shelter....

"A baby!" The senator's face got beet red. "Boy or girl?" he demanded, booming again. "How old? Got any pictures? M'youngest just had her second. A girl. Named her Madison, for pity's sake. Do you kids pick these confusin' names on purpose?"

"My son's name is Michael, Senator," she responded with a smile. "And he's a month old."

"Lord-a-mercy, child," the senator boomed. "Call me Elliston. And tell me everything. Is he sleepin' through the night yet?"

Dani knew her mouth was hanging open, but she couldn't help it. She'd never in a million years imagined that the powerful senator from Louisiana would be gaga over babies.

"We'll let Walker talk later," Perrodeaux promised lazily, "while we're loading up on Maryland crab cakes and the best dessert this side of Louisiana hummingbird cake."

"Sorry, Senator," Josh interrupted, wrapping his arm around Dani's shoulders in a possessive move that stirred her dreams and her hormones. "But there isn't a dessert on this earth that can match this woman's chocolate pie with mile-high meringue."

Perrodeaux took a sip of the bourbon and branch water the waiter had deposited in front of him. "My, my. I haven't had a decent slice of pie since my wife died ten years ago," he said reflectively. "My daughters are so busy between their careers and their kids, I don't think either one of them could boil an egg, let alone manage to produce an edible pie crust."

Dani smiled. "Surely you're exaggerating, Elliston. They feed their families somehow."

"Fast food, young lady," the senator barked. "Carryout. One of 'em even signed up with some service that does the cooking for her. She picks up a week's worth of dinners at a time, then all she does is throw something in the microwave every night."

I could do that, Dani thought, and elation flooded through her. *It's the perfect answer. Perfect.*

She beamed at Senator Perrodeaux. "Oh, Elliston, thank you! You've just solved—well, my future. And my son's. I'll be able to earn a living and raise Michael myself. Oh, you darling man, thank you!"

She leaned forward, exposing the creamy tops of her lush breasts to the entire world, and kissed the old bozo.

Josh growled.

Perrodeaux chuckled, his full cheeks flushed bright pink. "Now, honey," he drawled in that irritating good-ol'-boy accent. Reaching in his vest pocket, he pulled out a business card, produced a pen and scribbled something on the back. Handing it to her with a flourish, he said, "Always glad to help new mamas. Now that's my private line. You need anything—anything at all, don't hesitate to call. I've even got a great cure for colic."

Without missing a beat, the senior senator from Louisiana turned to Josh. "I hear you're somethin' of an expert on western range management practices. We've got some hearings on the subject comin' up soon and I could use some unbiased information."

He continued to pump Josh as they left the bar, were seated in the dining room and consumed a meal that was probably excellent by Washingtonian standards. So-so on the Caldwell scale.

Josh tried to answer the senator's questions to the best of his ability, but his attention was elsewhere.

Glued to his Texas angel in that sinfully attractive dress.

Finally he was thanking the senator, tipping the parking valet and hustling Dani into the car. Driving off. Stopping in a secluded spot where they could watch the lights of Washington sparkle like floating diamonds on the dark waters of the Potomac.

"Josh?" Dani asked as he shut off the ignition and slid his arm slowly, casually, along the seat back. "What are we doing here?"

Getting lucky? He should be so lucky. "Just taking a few minutes to transition from politics to diapers."

Dani giggled. "I can't believe I was afraid to meet Senator Perrodeaux. I'm sorry if he talked more about babies than your environmental views."

"No problem," Josh assured her. "I just want to add my two cents to the process. Thanks to you, tonight, I have the chance."

"I didn't—"

He couldn't let her discount her role in the night's success, but he didn't want to argue. So he kissed her.

Somewhere in the firestorm of desire, he wondered if it would always be this way between them. Thought it might be. Wanted to spend a few decades finding out.

Dani reveled in his mouth on hers. This was what she wanted more than anything. Josh holding her. Kissing her. Letting her kiss him.

She gave herself up to the sheer passion and pleasure. Just for a few moments, she'd live the dream. She'd be Josh's woman. He'd be her man. Showing her how much he needed her.

Their mouths mated, the kisses deepened. His tongue

sought entrance, driving inside, filling, tasting, exploring, tempting. Being tasted, explored, tempted.

"Oh, Dani," Josh murmured, his breath warm against her skin, his hands and mouth everywhere, sending shivers of desire and joy tumbling through her. "You're so beautiful. I want…" His hand curved lovingly around her breast, taking its weight in his palm. His thumb stroked the crest. He moaned. A low answering sound came from her throat.

"Stay," he whispered, fulfilling the dream she wanted most to come true. A future with the man she'd come to love as much as she loved Michael.

"Oh, Josh," she breathed. "I…I don't—"

"Just for a while," he said quickly. "Not forever. Just, uh, we could see how it goes.…"

Dani's eyes stung, but she'd be damned if she'd cry. *I gave tears up years ago,* she reminded herself, *because they don't change anything. They certainly can't change a proposition into a proposal.*

"Speaking of going," she said stiffly, dragging herself from his seductive embrace. "It's late. I think you'd better take me home."

"But—"

"It's past time for Michael's feeding," she said evenly, adopting his toneless response to unwanted emotions.

Josh didn't start the car right away. Just sat there looking at the shimmering platinum ribbons of light on black water, his hands white-knuckled on the steering wheel. "Dani, I'm sorry," he said through gritted teeth. "That wasn't fair. F-forget I even brought up the subject."

He released the steering wheel and cranked the starter.

Well, he wasn't going to sit around and argue with her. If she didn't want to stay forever, it was better if she left soon. Before she took his heart and his future with her.…

They drove home in total silence. Until they reached the security gates.

Which were wide-open. "What the—" Josh pulled the car slowly through, cruised down the main street, turned at their corner and drove—

Into hell. Again.

This time it had eerie, flashing lights and thick smoke. Fire trucks, police cars and emergency vehicles parked at every imaginable angle. Small clumps of spectators in night-clothes. And hose lines, like fat, gray worms, snaking every which way.

He'd slowed the car to a crawl, still trying to work out what was happening, when Dani gave a cry, then leaped from the car and sprinted away into the darkness past his headlights.

Josh braked. Craned his neck to see where she— He wrenched the key to turn off the engine. Flew out of the car. Ran full-out. Catching up with Dani, he grabbed her shoulders and hung on for support, just as they reached Marletta, who was propped against the side of a fire truck, with a blanket around her shoulders and an oxygen mask over her face.

"Are you okay?" he asked.

When she nodded wearily, Josh asked the question that Dani's searching gaze was frantically trying to answer.

"Wh-where's Michael?"

Chapter Eight

"Michael's over th-there," Marletta rasped, pointing past a clot of emergency vehicles to an ambulance unit before wiping her streaming eyes with a crumpled tissue. "He—" A bout of coughing stopped her before she could finish the sentence.

Please, Dani prayed as a firestorm of fear scorched through her. *Please don't take my son.*

Yet even as she reeled under the excruciating pain of that possibility, Dani suddenly understood how Josh—and Jimmy's parents—could react so extremely when faced with a child's death. Losing a spouse was hard enough—even when he'd already become a stranger—but a child...

A child, no matter how old, held a parent's heart hostage. Nothing could ever ease the sorrow of such a loss.

When this is over and Michael is fine, Dani thought, forcing herself to think positively, to breathe slowly and wait for Marletta to finish before racing off to find her baby, *I'll send Jimmy's parents a long letter and some pictures of their grandson. Tell them I understand their grief now. Try to work out a compromise so they can be part of Michael's life. Unless something terrible—*

No. She wouldn't borrow trouble. She didn't dare.

"Take your time, Marletta." Josh's deep voice came from a spot above and behind Dani's ear just as his big, strong hands wrapped around her shoulders.

She could hear the barely leashed tension in his voice as he went on. "Do you need oxygen or something? Some water?"

Without thinking about it, Dani reached up and covered his hands with her own.

The secretary shook her head. "Give me—" She held up one finger as another spasm of coughing racked her.

Dani leaned back, her fear made manageable only by Josh's solid presence. Once again she needed his strength to survive a dreadful ordeal. And once again he was there. Just as he had been when Michael was born. She pressed against his hard chest, grateful, so grateful that she didn't have to face this devastating shock alone.

Finally, Marletta got her lungs cleared enough to say, "The paramedics insisted on checking him out—" The tissue gestured toward the ambulance. "But he *was* breathing when I brought him out."

"Thank God..." Dani let out the breath she'd been holding and turned to go, but the secretary held up her hand, palm out.

"Walker...Dani..." Marletta dabbed at her eyes again, hitched up the blanket draped over her shoulders. "I..."

Dani fought down her need to charge off in search of Michael. She knew the E.M.T.'s were giving her son every possible care—and it was clear that Marletta *needed* to say something first.

"Spit it out, Langtry," Josh barked. "What the hell happened?"

Dani twisted her head to look at him. *Oh, no.* Warrior mode again. His hands curled into fists on his hips, his jaw carved granite, Josh was surveying the scene like a conquering lord prioritizing the pillaging. Big jerk—not even noticing his secretary's light coffee-colored skin had a definite gray cast to it.

Well, that resolved Dani's lingering indecision. As long as she knew Michael was alive, she could spare a minute or two to protect the woman who'd saved him. She wasn't leaving Marletta here alone to deal with Josh. Not this way. Not now.

"Apparently, the town house on the end caught fire," the older woman began. "The firefighter who gave me oxygen said they contained the fire to that unit, but the smoke traveled through the entire building along the attic space." She turned large, dark, still-streaming eyes in Dani's direction. "Oh, Dani, I feel so terrible!"

"Marletta, please. What happened to Michael?" Josh persisted tonelessly. The cool voice, so at odds with his hot fingers once again pressing on her shoulders like metal vise grips, sent a shiver down Dani's already chilled spine.

After another spasm of coughing, Marletta gulped, then answered. "Well, he fussed a little over the bottle." She smiled tentatively at Dani. "Of course, he would, since he's used to his mama."

Hoping to lessen the woman's concern and speed her story before Josh exploded, Dani returned the smile.

"I finally got him to sleep," Marletta continued, "and went downstairs to watch TV." She wiped at her eyes again. "By the time I smelled something and went to investigate...the smoke was pretty thick. I grabbed Michael and got out as fast as I could, but..." Wringing her hands, she rushed the rest of the words out. "I don't know how long he was up there breathing that horrible black stuff. The paramedics said they thought he'd be okay, but I'll...I'll never forgive myself if...if anything... Oh, I should have stayed up there with him! Please—forgive me?"

Impulsively, Dani reached over and gave Marletta a com-

forting squeeze. The fire certainly wasn't her fault, but—
would Josh blame the woman for doing the best she could
in a bad situation? He'd done it before....

Dani chewed her lip as she moved away from Josh's embrace and turned to watch his reaction to Marletta's plea.

After a long moment Josh touched the older woman's
shoulder awkwardly.

"Nothing to forgive," he said, the briskness of his
clipped tone at odds with his warm smile. "You volunteered
to baby-sit, not to escape disaster. Who knows, if Dani and
I had been home, we might have been upstairs asleep, too.
Been overcome by smoke along with Michael. We might
have all died."

He's right, Dani thought while Josh made sure that Marletta could get home okay. If they hadn't gone to dinner
with the senator tonight, the fire still would have started.
Could she or Josh have done any better than Marletta did
in getting herself and Michael to safety?

Bad things can happen. To anyone. Anytime. Without
warning.

Dani shook off the negative thought. Good can come
from bad, she reminded herself. She'd ended up with Michael, after all. And met Josh.

And she'd never regret either experience, no matter how
short a time they lasted.

The only thing a person could do about life was be prepared to accept whatever happened, pick up the pieces and
build anew.

So why let a few setbacks stop your dreaming? asked her
braver self, the self that still hoped despite all fear.

Tonight's crisis made it clear that she had to make arrangements for Michael's future that took the unexpected
into account. If something happened to her, who would raise
Michael? Jimmy's parents were his only other relatives.

So she'd work out the details of this meals-for-busy-
people business and she'd work hard to make it a success.

She'd also make arrangements for the Caldwells to meet Michael.

If she could arrange it safely. She might be undergoing a change of heart and perspective, but she wasn't crazy enough to risk losing her son permanently. At least, not to vindictive grandparents. Not without taking a few legal precautions first.

Life itself was enough of a gamble.

And every moment of love precious. Dani uttered a low moan of impatience and began edging in the direction of the ambulance where her son was being treated. She needed to hold Michael. Now!

Josh looked wistfully toward the conglomeration of emergency vehicles before turning back to his secretary. "I'll stay with you until you feel well enough to head for home, but I'm sure Dani wants to check on Michael."

"No, no. I'll be fine," Marletta insisted, making shooing gestures with her tissue. "Y'all go on."

It didn't take any more persuasion. Dani plunged into the crowd of milling firefighters, police, and sundry onlookers. Josh gave Marletta a quick hug, then took off after her, determined to hold it together as long as Dani and Michael needed him.

Then he planned to go somewhere quiet and have a nice, complete nervous breakdown.

Some dope in a law enforcement uniform tried to halt his forward progress; Josh tossed him aside. "Get the hell out of my way," he explained. "I'm looking for my baby."

"He seems to be okay now, ma'am," the paramedic was saying when Josh finally reached Dani. "So we'll release him to you."

"Thank you," she whispered, gazing down at the baby she held tightly. Michael was wrapped in his own crib blanket, Josh noted absently as he reached over Dani's shoulder to touch him. He needed the contact. Needed to skim his hand over the infant's fuzzy hair, his little arms, those tiny toes tucked safely inside the blanket. Just to reassure himself.

"Smoke inhalation in infants this small can be tricky, though," the paramedic continued as he slung his stethoscope around his neck and tucked the listening end into his shirt pocket. "It's possible he may develop residual breathing difficulties in the next twenty-four hours."

"And i-if he does?" Dani asked haltingly.

"Get him to a hospital for inhalation therapy."

Josh stood directly behind Dani. Bracing her back with his chest, pretending to lend her his support again. *The same way you did during Michael's delivery?* he asked himself derisively. *Gonna get whoozy this time, too?*

No, by God. This time, he was going to be useful. "Which one's the best?" Josh asked.

"Well, All Saints is nearby. It has a good pediatric staff, good reputation."

The E.M.T.'s radio squawked. "Listen, I think the little guy'll be fine," he said in a brisk professional tone. "You might prop him up for the rest of the night. That'll keep his airway open with minimal strain.

"He definitely ate some smoke, though. That can depress the appetite, so if he's not too hungry tonight, don't worry about it.

"He should be just fine in a day or two. He's a good, strong kid. Cute, too." The paramedic ruffled Michael's pale fluffy hair and grinned at Josh and Dani. "You two make good babies," he said, then turned to murmur something to his companion and start packing up his equipment.

"Thanks again," Dani called to the paramedic as he climbed into the back of the ambulance to stow the gear. "Thank you so much for saving my son."

There it was again. *Her* son.

Dammit, Michael was *his* baby, too.

Something was going to have to be done about that. And soon.

He'd claim eminent domain. Emotional investment. Something.

Wrapping one arm around Dani's to help support Michael, Josh mused on the twists of fate. Dinner with a national power broker and some hot kisses hadn't seemed to make much of an impression on his Texas angel—judging by the way she'd jumped on that drive-by food idea—but this fire might buy him a little more time. Delay her departure for entrepreneur land until they were sure Michael had completely recovered from tonight's trauma.

Maybe he could talk her into staying long enough to help him repaint the upstairs. Or maybe, if he was really lucky, the building would be condemned and he'd need help finding a house and moving in and by the time they got that accomplished, she'd be in the habit of—

Scheme later, Walker. Right now, you've got more pressing tasks to accomplish. Because even if she won't let you keep her and Michael permanently, you can take care of them tonight.

First and foremost, they needed shelter. That was simple logistics. He could handle it.

Giving Dani strict orders not to leave the spot, and crossing his fingers in hopes she'd actually do it, Josh went to discover their options.

Not many. Nobody was being allowed back into any part of the building until it had been inspected for structural soundness. Which meant they'd either have to sleep in the old station wagon or...

"Come on, honey," he said when he found her again, near the car. "Let's get Michael out of here."

Dani obeyed numbly. She'd felt drained, emotionally and physically, before they'd even arrived home to face this nightmarish scene; now she was totally incapable of the simplest decision. She only wanted to sit and hold Michael and savor the fact that he was still alive.

Life's a risky business every day. Even for children.

Which just means there's no time to waste.

Her dreams weren't very big, but if she wanted them to come true—and she did, because tonight's near-disaster reminded her that life without dreams was merely existence—she should pursue them.

Attaining her dreams was her responsibility, after all.

So was accepting reality.

She loved Josh Walker, wanted him...but she needed him forever or not at all.

He'd kissed her senseless in the moonlight, but he hadn't offered permanency in any form.

So that made her life—and her future—simple again.

She'd put aside the dream of a loving husband with turquoise eyes, concentrate on achieving the rest of her goals alone, and learn to be satisfied with that.

Tonight, though, Michael had narrowly escaped death. So for a few short hours she'd let herself pretend fantasy was real. She'd let Josh put on his masterful act, helping her and Michael into the car, driving to an all-night grocery to buy diapers, baby wipes and a package of infant T-shirts, then booking them into a nearby bed-and-breakfast recommended by the grocery clerk.

The man was simply phenomenal when it came to putting kindness and care into action.

Within thirty minutes of leaving his town house, Josh turned onto a gravel drive that led to—another of Dani's dreams. The perfect setting for the honeymoon she'd always imagined but never had. A classic, Southern plantation-style mansion sat on a rise above a lake, looking like a multitiered wedding cake. White columns soaring two stories high and railings edging the wide porch gleamed like frosting in the light of a full moon. An ornate, wrought iron light fixture hung over the extra-wide front door with a traditional fan-light window above it.

Josh apologized to the owners for rousing them so late, explained their situation briefly and accepted without protest the only accommodation available. One room. One bed.

More dream material, Dani thought as they were escorted to their room. A beautiful, canopied four-poster bed. Twelve-foot ceiling. Heart-pine floor. Carved cherrywood armoire and settee. A huge bouquet of lilacs and statice and antique roses perfumed the air.

Oh, yes, it was the perfect setting for a honeymoon.

And Josh the perfect groom.

Except he wasn't her husband. He wasn't *her* anything.

And I need to remember that, accept that. Even if I don't like it.

Dani sank onto the spindle-back chair beside the fireplace and couldn't stop a tear from trickling down her cheek.

Then Josh was on his knees in front of her, lifting Michael from her arms and wiping away the tear with his thumb. "Shh, sweetheart," he whispered in a low voice that sent comforting warmth all the way to her core. "It's okay. You're worn out, that's all. Michael's alive and it'll all be better in the morning."

Standing, Josh deposited the baby on the bed, then stripped off his suit jacket and tie and let them drop. Un-buckled his belt and loosened the waistband of his trousers. Kicked off his shoes as he unbuttoned his shirt. Handing her the shirt, he escorted her to the bathroom, told her to undress and use the shirt as a nightgown.

When she reappeared a few minutes later, looking un-bearably sexy with the shirttails around her knees and the cuffs folded back several times, Josh excused himself to take a quick—cold—shower while she nursed Michael.

Who wasn't hungry, just as the E.M.T. had warned them, he reminded Dani as he killed the lights and slid into bed.

They propped Michael up between them on a stack of pillows.

See? Another dream come true... Dani told herself wryly as she inhaled Josh's clean, piney scent that clung to the pima cotton shirt wrapped around her. *You're sleeping with the most gorgeous male animal you've ever known.*

He's also the kindest, gruffest, sexiest, silliest...

Her eyes drifted closed in the middle of her litany.

Barely conscious, she felt a movement on the bed. Josh's hand gently burrowed under her palm where it rested on Michael's leg; his strong fingers entwined with hers and his breathing deepened and slowed.

With a sigh of thanksgiving, Dani checked Michael once more, made a note to call Marletta in the morning...and let herself drop into the well of sleep.

He couldn't figure out what woke him. Didn't know where he was for a minute.

Then a silhouette wearing a man's shirt moved past the bed and he heard the sound again.

It was a baby gasping for breath and it drove fear straight through his heart into his soul.

"What— How is he?" Josh asked, throwing back the fancy bedding and planting his feet on the floor. Ready for action, hoping none was required.

"N-not g-good." Dani's attempt at control was about as sorry as his pretense of coolness under pressure.

"Then you should have waked me, dammit!" Josh barked, turning his fear to anger, just as he'd turned his anger at Carrie to icy numbness. "Get dressed," he ordered, scrambling in the darkness to find his clothes. "We're taking him to All Saints."

It had been easier to slip through life untouched, like an iceberg floating in the sea, he thought as he grabbed his slacks and began pulling them on.

But he couldn't do it. Not anymore. Michael and his

mother had melted that ice permanently. Stripped him defenseless against these damned, terrible feelings. Worry. Fear. Helplessness.

Joy and desire, too, he reminded himself as he took Michael and waved Dani toward her clothes. He'd never soared to such heights on one woman's kiss. Never been brought to the very brink of passion with one look from a pair of wide, green eyes.

And never felt such tender, almost painful joy just from holding an innocent child in his arms.

A child now laboring for every breath.

"I don't have any insurance," Dani said, modesty forgotten as she pulled on her dress, zipped it, then handed Josh his shirt. She tried to manipulate her foot into a strappy high-heel, then abandoned the attempt. "We'd better go to the county hospital."

Like hell. "The paramedic said All Saints is the best, so that's where we're going," Josh said. Well, okay. Maybe he snarled it. But this was Michael they were talking about.

"And if they turn us away?" She snarled right back. Good. If she cratered, he would, too. "This is no time to gamble with Michael's life."

"Exactly." Josh snatched the car keys off the nightstand, jammed his shirttails into his pants and his wallet into his back pocket, shoved his bare feet into his shoes and draped his suit coat over Dani's shoulders, then jerked open the bedroom door. "So let's move! Nobody's going to worry about finances when a baby's life is at stake."

Right.

"I'm sorry," the battle-ax behind the high counter drawled, fingering the collar of her lavender smock. "Really."

With a thin, phony smile and cold iron in her voice, she went on. "I don't make the rules, sir. And as I said—twice now, I believe—All Saints requires proof of insur—"

"We. Don't. Have. Insurance!" Josh shouted. "What we have is a baby who's…who's…" He buried his fingers in his hair, struggling to hold on to his temper, for Michael's sake.

His baby needed treatment and, by God, this hospital *would* treat him.

He'd driven Dani's old clunker like an Indy car through the predawn deserted streets. Just so this smug bureaucrat could turn them away? No freaking way.

Michael was trying to cry and couldn't…couldn't get his breath. His face was red and tear-streaked; he struggled weakly in his mother's arms.

Dammit! What was wrong with this woman? With a growl, Josh thrust frustrated fingers through his hair again.

Dani slipped between him and the admissions desk. Her scent filled his nostrils. Her hair streamed loose down her back and spilled over his arm as she handed Michael to him.

"We'd like to see your supervisor, Ms.—" Dani leaned forward to read the ID badge clipped to the woman's smock "—Sapperstein. Now!"

With a disdainful sniff, the clerk disappeared through a door behind her.

Josh's tension level dropped half a point. "What are you planning to say to the border guard's supervisor?" he asked with a wry, only semiforced smile. His Texas angel had bedeviled Bubba. She'd whip this hospital, too.

"I'm not going to say anything if I can help it," Dani replied, reclaiming Michael. "You're the legal expert. I'm counting on you to start muttering about lawsuits and…"

What was left of his composure threatened to disappear at her act of trust. Misplaced trust, it appeared. He felt like David taking on Goliath—without his slingshot.

But Dani needed him.

And she was looking at him with her green angel eyes wide and clear. Shadowless.

His heart swelled, exploded in his chest. Lordy, bring

back the dragon in the lavender smock. He was ready to do some serious slaying.

With one trembling finger, he touched Dani's cheek. "I won't let you down," he promised when he could get words past his tonsils.

Ms. Sapperstein appeared in the doorway behind the admissions desk. A bespectacled, bow-tied man followed her.

"Okay, darlin', watch this," Josh said in quiet, firm tones as the bureaucrats approached. He gave Dani a reassuring smile. Whatever it took, Michael would get the treatment he needed. He couldn't put another shadow in her forest eyes.

As she eyed the bow tie-wearer, Dani placed a restraining hand on his arm. "Josh? Don't yell—unless you have to."

"Spoilsport." He touched her cheek again, rubbed his thumb lightly across her lush lower lip. Then turned to the smug little admissions clerk and her boss. "I'm Josh Walker," he stated grimly, turning his fear for Michael's welfare into icy resolve. "And I hope I misunderstood Ms. Sapperstein when she attempted to refuse emergency treatment to a child."

"Edgar Beldon," the bow tie replied, adding primly, "And I hope *you* understand that All Saints is not a charity hospital."

Josh ran a hand through his hair as he counted to ten. By God, after he got the environment cleaned up, he was going to fix the medical services delivery system in this country.

"That infant—" Josh said, pointed toward Dani, who now held Michael upright in front of her "—suffered smoke inhalation last night and began experiencing breathing difficulties about forty-five minutes ago."

Beldon touched the bridge of his eyeglasses. "He doesn't appear to be in imminent danger. Without insurance, the—"

"That's it," Josh declared, and reached across the counter to grab Beldon by his bow tie. Pulled the weasely paperpusher forward until their faces were only inches apart.

Using his free hand to pull out his wallet, Josh tossed it on the counter. "I may still sue your as—institution, but in the interest of saving time, I am prepared to offer you unfeeling vultures something better than insurance," he said with a wolfish smile that had the bureaucrat squirming. "Money."

Finally. He'd found the magic word.

Within minutes the lavender-smocked bat was summoning a pediatric care nurse from the respiratory unit.

"Here." She shoved a clipboard holding a sheaf of forms at him just as the nurse arrived. "These forms must be filled out completely and returned to the cashier's office before the patient can be discharged."

"I'll fill them out later," Josh said, trying to shove the clipboard back at the admissions clerk. "Right now, I'm going with them." He motioned toward Dani, who'd handed Michael to the nurse in fuchsia and was following her back down the corridor.

"I don't care where you fill them out," Ms. Sapperstein retorted. Then she smiled. "And I'm glad you insisted on seeing Mr. Beldon. I hate to turn away babies, but...my hands are tied."

As Josh accepted her apology with a mumbled thanks and headed after Dani, the woman called, "Good luck with your son."

He is mine—in all the ways that count.

Josh hurried down the hall after Dani. Her shoulders were drawn in—as if bracing for a blow. Her fingers were curled into fists, but that didn't stop their trembling. He knew without seeing it that her teeth were chewing on her lip.

He caught up just in time to hear the nurse say, "Exposure to certain chemical emissions can cause permanent brain damage in infants this young if their respiratory systems are immature. Do you know if there were any hazardous materials in the fire? Asbestos or—"

"How soon will we see the doctor?" Josh interrupted the

doomsayer. Capturing Dani's hand, he gave it a reassuring squeeze.

Now more than ever, she needed him. But not the gut-knotting fear or panicky helplessness raging through him.

So he shoved them behind a wall of ice. The way he had imprisoned himself in his anger for six years. At last, his suffering served a useful purpose—helping the living survive one more frightful experience.

"We've already paged him," the nurse said, pointing them to a waiting area before whirling Michael away to a room filled with high-tech gizmos.

The waiting area, empty of people at this predawn hour, contained a blaring television, some ancient reading material, and a narrow window letting in bronzy parking lot light.

They waited silently. Holding hands.

Shortly after sunrise an energetic young doctor burst into their alcove, dragged them off to a torture chamber—he called it a neonatal respiratory treatment unit—and fired a couple thousand questions at first Dani, then Josh. After refusing to answer any of *their* questions, the young quack dismissed them abruptly and bent over Michael's chart, muttering to himself. The baby lay on his side in a Plexiglas box, fussing and bewildered—but alive.

They waited some more. Josh kept his sanity—barely—by focusing on the one meaningful thing he could do: take care of Dani. He found some vending machines and brought her a juice drink, made her eat something purported to be a breakfast burrito. Bullied the nursing staff into cooperating when Dani's milk…well, overflowed.

Hours crawled by. The shift changed. The aides, orderlies and floor clerks bustling past wore different colored uniforms, at least.

Josh didn't know. Didn't care. He just wanted news of Michael. Good news.

It didn't come and Josh realized *this* was hell. Really hell. Because he couldn't fix whatever was wrong. Couldn't stop loving Michael and walk away, either. Simply had to sit here, helplessly suffering through this.

But not alone.

He couldn't have done this alone.

He *wouldn't* do it for anyone but Michael. And Dani.

Not even Carrie and the child lost to him six years ago.

It hit him then. First like lightning striking a tree, blasting the bark off it in great strips. Then...after that initial shock of recognition, the knowledge seemed more like a deep layer of rock—solid, immutable, eons old.

He loved Dani. His beautiful Texas angel, who brought out the best in him. He loved Michael, too. Wanted to be his father for life—even if the price was endless rounds of this debilitating worry and fear, years of lost sleep over the nameless perils of daily living....

He wouldn't go through fatherhood for anyone else. Or with anyone but Dani.

She and Michael were his second chance. He needed them to heal his heart, to give his life meaning.

They were his.

Until they leave.

No! Josh leaped from his chair, the sports section of yesterday's newspaper that he'd been pretending to read falling from his hand. They had to stay. And not just for a few more weeks.

"What?" Dani cried, alarmed by his sudden movement. "What is it?"

"Oh, uh...I—I thought I saw the doc," he said.

"No." She shook her head as a sigh escaped. "I've been watching. He hasn't come back from the other wing yet."

Josh looked as if he wanted to say something more, but after a moment he shrugged those broad shoulders and subsided onto the padded vinyl seat again.

Nothing happened for another interminable hour.

The waiting—with cold dread knotting her stomach and helpless fear immobilizing every muscle—became familiar.

Was familiar. She'd lived with similar terror gripping her like a tiger's talons during Jimmy's final hours in the hospital.

She wanted to scream and throw things, of course, but she knew how useless that would be. So, instead, she folded her hands in her lap and kept waiting.

"How can you be so calm?" Josh growled suddenly.

Because you're with me. She would never have survived these hours of helpless waiting without Josh's solid strength and steadfast care.

Right after the doctor had dismissed them, Josh had even let her press her face to the shirt covering his hard, muscular chest and cry tears that didn't change anything—although getting them out made her feel better.

Dani glanced at Josh. Holding each other didn't seem to make him feel better, though.

His jaw was granite again, his handsome features darkened into a scowling mask—he didn't look exactly comforted.

"As long as he's alive, there's hope," she insisted.

"I... God help me," he whispered brokenly, running his hand over his unshaven jaw. His golden hair was disheveled, his turquoise eyes suspiciously moist. "I want to be strong for you, Dani. For you and Michael, but I...I don't know how much more I can take!"

He stood and began pacing the waiting area, his hands thrust deep into the pockets of his rumpled dress slacks. "All those years I lived with the pain of losing the child Carrie denied me and it was...only an idea that never got a chance to become real.

"But, Michael... I've held him, bathed him, played with him. I know how he smells. I've rocked him to sleep.... Oh, Dani, what if— I mean— God, Dani, how do people survive this? Even if he's okay this time, kids just keep..."

"Being kids," Dani finished for him with a rueful smile.

"That's the problem with life. It's dangerous." And always too short.

And only love made it worth the struggle.

She looked into the depths of her companion's tired, concerned turquoise eyes and couldn't sugarcoat reality for him. Or for herself, either. "But bad things can happen, Josh. Dreams die. P-people die. Even chil—"

"Shh." Josh pressed her head into the angle between his neck and his shoulder, held her while she soaked his shirt again. "Whatever happens," he promised, "we'll handle it together."

And that was all anyone could ask for. Someone to share the joy and the pain, the hope and the fear that measure life.

The only someone she wanted was the man she'd fallen in love with, the man she couldn't have. Josh Walker.

"Are you Michael Caldwell's parents?" A youngster in a labcoat stood before them.

"Yes." They both stood and Dani clasped Josh's hand. "How...how is he?" Josh asked, his fingers squeezing hers.

The kid fiddled with her stethoscope. "I'm Dr. Davila," she announced, then smiled. "And Michael is hungry."

Josh almost fainted with relief. Dani hugged the doctor—who grinned. "We also think he's lactose intolerant," she said, leading them out of the waiting area. "The smoke exposure makes it difficult to be absolutely sure without additional tests, but—"

"You mean, he's allergic to milk?" Josh asked as he halted both women in front of the crowded central nursing station.

"Cow's milk," Dr. Davila amended, still grinning. "Seems to be flourishing on mother's. We suggest you have him tested at a later—"

Josh quit listening. Michael was okay.

He picked Dani up and kissed her. Soared to heaven as usual—right there with an All Saints audience.

Chapter Nine

"**Y**ou have to stop doing that," Dani said shakily some forty minutes later as they drove away from the hospital.

"What?" Josh grinned. He couldn't help himself. A gloriously healthy Michael slept in his car seat. And Michael's mother had participated enthusiastically in their embrace, at least for a while.

"Kissing me," Dani answered. "Especially in public. It— People might get the wrong idea."

"Whatever you say, honey," Josh agreed absently as his favorite fantasy floated across his consciousness. Dani, above him, her magnificent hair tumbling free, brushing over his...

She's not going to marry you to fulfill your *fantasies, doofus,* he reminded himself sternly.

"I'm not your honey, either, Josh."

Her protest sounded more tired than angry, and he wasn't ready to argue the issue now, anyway.

Soon, though. Very soon. When the right moment came along, Josh intended to propose.

Meanwhile he mumbled something placatory, then

dropped her and Michael off at the bed-and-breakfast with orders to rest, and headed for the office to grab the extra set of court-appearance clothes he kept there. Got caught again by phone calls from Cleveland.

After supporting the telecom industry for a couple of hours, Josh returned to the Colonial mansion and caught a nap while Dani and the owners sat on the front porch, schmoozing about breakfast casseroles. That evening, he took Dani and the miraculous Michael shopping for a few necessities, since they were still barred from the town house.

The B and B owners agreed to let them stay another night—in separate rooms, dammit. The following day was spent supervising the professional cleaning crew provided by the town homes' management. Even Josh knew that wasn't the right time or place for a proposal.

And the next damned day, he was summoned to court on some stupid landmark case.

Damn these federal judges with their sweeping powers and their lousy timing. He needed to propose! To offer...

What, big shot? Josh asked himself as he sat in his office brooding the afternoon away. Reinholdt had called an indefinite recess so he could research a citation the defendant's mouthpiece had tossed in to support some spurious objection.

He wanted Dani and Michael in his life. Permanently.

That left just one little, tiny problem, though. How to make *them* want *him* around full-time.

Hey—persuasion's my game, he reminded himself as his excitement—and its male corollary—began rising. As usual. *I just have to put together an offer she can't refuse.*

Josh rubbed a hand thoughtfully over his jaw. He needed something more than promises as an enticement, though. Dani certainly knew that promises could be broken.

He'd better offer something other than love, too. She'd had that. And after all these years of stupid, bitter refusal to feel anything, maybe he wouldn't be very good at lov-

ing—even a woman as special as Dani. His experience with
Carrie had certainly taught him that willingness wasn't
enough.

Stick to tangibles, then.

Let's see... He had a house and furnishings that still
reeked of smoke. A postage-stamp backyard that wasn't big
enough for a toddler, let alone a kid—who'd soon need a
decent-size dog, too. And he drove an old car that, even
though it ran like a top now, was, well...cosmetically chal-
lenged.

Josh looked around the office, vainly hoping to see something, anything, that indicated he had a quality or two that
Dani might value.

His spirits sank. Nothing but debris.

Picking up the nearest coffee cup, he peered inside.
Jeez—there was gray-green fuzz growing on the bottom of
it. Grimacing, he put it down, wondering if the second
chance Dani's rescue had given him had any chance at all.

*Face it, Walker, you're not much of a bargain as a hus-
band. You can't blame Dani if her current interests revolve
around Michael and cooking for strangers.*

Well, okay, he'd do the best he could and hope it was
good enough.

He'd try to be neater and he'd find a house with a big
yard for Michael and a big kitchen for her. He'd trade the
clunker for a van and do whatever else he could to help
Dani get that feed-the-workaholics business off the ground.

Or stay home and raise Michael. Whatever she wanted.

Of course, he wanted as many of Dani's kids as she'd
give him and the very concept of conceiving them with her
made him hard. But he wouldn't ask for another baby. He
didn't need one. Not as long as he could be around—with
Dani—while Michael grew up.

Dammit, he *needed* Dani. To give his life meaning. To
flavor his days. To heat his nights.

He'd do everything in his power to make her happy. And

he'd love her with every beat of the heart she and Michael had healed—

Josh sighed. He just didn't think it would be enough. Most women wanted some romance with their marriage and he didn't have the slightest idea how to be romantic. Maybe he could call his sister-in-law for some pointers. Annie would help him out—once she stopped laughing herself silly....

With a frustrated growl, Josh moved a pile of articles on grassland reclamation costs so he could drum his fingers on the cleared desktop space. What he really needed was some...*leverage.*

How about a trip to Paris for our honeymoon, so she can enroll in that world-famous blue cooking school?

Marletta appeared in the doorway, wearing her school principal's frown.

"What?" he asked, frowning back. Dammit, he'd asked not to be disturbed for anything short of a judicial summons, which he really didn't expect until tomorrow. Cases in Reinholdt's court always dragged.

"Could be nothing," the secretary said slowly as she rearranged her latest red pencil in her hair. "Or it could be trouble."

Josh waggled his eyebrows to indicate that she go on.

Marletta jerked a thumb backward over her shoulder. "Man just walked in looking for you. I've never seen him before."

Deepening the frown to a scowl, Josh said, "So? If he's a new client, do a preliminary interview and tell him we'll get back to him." Couldn't she see he was trying to formulate an irresistible proposal here?

"Uh-uh." Marletta shook her head emphatically. "In fact, he seemed surprised to discover that you're an attorney. Said his name was Graves."

That made it Josh's turn to shake his head. "Doesn't ring

a bell," he said flatly. "And if he's not looking for a lawyer, what's he want to see me about?"

Marletta crossed her arms over her chest. "He wouldn't say," she declared. "He *said* it was personal—" Leaning forward, she continued in a conspiratorial tone that would have made the CIA jealous. "*And* he's got a Texas accent!"

Ramifications sprinted through Josh's brain like tourists running before the bulls in Pamplona. He grinned. "I always said you were more observant than satellite surveillance. Show the gentleman in, Ms. Langtry."

Marletta looked stunned. "But—"

"If we've leaped to the right conclusions, this is bonus, baby." He smirked at his clever insertion of a new slang term. And at his unexpected good fortune. "Show Mr. Graves in," he repeated as he stood and buttoned his collar button with one hand while snagging his suit jacket with the other. "So I can show him right back out. Then I'm going home and getting engaged. A.S.A.P.—I hope."

"Well! It's about time you wised up," Marletta said, lips quirking. "Your visitor talks pretty slow with that Texas drawl, though. Think you can send him on his way in less than twenty minutes?"

Josh jerked the knot on his tie tight and smoothed the ends as he came around his desk and herded his secretary toward the outer office. "Time me," he suggested.

It took seventeen minutes. Just long enough for Graves, a lanky, rawboned man in his early fifties whose cowboy boots, string tie and Stetson declared his origin before he opened his mouth, to show Josh his private investigator's license and explain that he'd been hired by Pete and Edna Caldwell to locate their daughter-in-law, Danielle.

"I traced her to West Texas 'bout a month ago," Graves said with a twang. "Little town name o' No Lake. I think she saw a doctor there, but nobody at the clinic'll tell me anything. Motel clerk linked her up with a Joshua Walker from Virginia. B'lieve that's you.''

The man was slick. Without giving Josh a chance to confirm or deny the connection, Graves laconically asked where Dani was at present.

"No idea," Josh said blithely. Well, hell, he wasn't on the witness stand and besides—she *might* be in the park, *might* be at the grocery store.... "Sorry. I can't help you."

Graves made a few more attempts to weasel information out of him, uttering glib assurances that the Caldwells no longer sought legal custody of their grandbaby but just wanted to contact their daughter-in-law. When Josh continued to stonewall, the Texan finally resettled his cowboy hat, adjusted the gold plate masquerading as his belt buckle, then pulled out a business card and penciled the Caldwells' phone number on the back before handing it over.

"I wasn't born yesterday, son," he drawled as he ambled toward the exit. "I noticed you ain't denied you know young Ms. Caldwell. So if you recall anythin' 'bout her whereabouts, I'd 'preciate it if you'd give me or the Caldwells a call. Day or night. They just want to be sure their grandbaby got here all right and that he—or she—has everythin' he needs."

That's going to be my job, Josh retorted silently. *Even if Dani won't have me as her husband. Because I am Michael's father in every essential way. Parent-child bonds are woven of shared history and heartstrings, not DNA chains.*

Graves broke into his reflections. "The Caldwells lost their only son, Mr. Walker. They're worried sick something mighta gone wrong with the only grandchild they're ever gonna have. You ken understand their concern, cain't ya?"

Josh looked down at his hands pressed flat against the desktop. Oh, yeah, he understood. He'd spent the past six years letting the same kind of obsessive thinking run his life, destroying any chance of happiness.

Of course, without Dani, he knew now, he couldn't have

He paused in the doorway to gaze adoringly at her. Little wisps of sunlit-brandy hair curling against her silky skin. Huge green eyes sparkling like rain-dampened moss. Full, sensual lips curving in a smile of sweet welcome. "God, you're beautiful," he breathed.

"And you're crazy," Dani said with a giggle to cover the ache of wishing he meant it. The contrast between his sleek, Virginia sophistication and her rural Lufkin roots was never clearer than right now.

Because some soot and smoke smell lingered—despite the horde of professionals who'd swept through the place yesterday, Dani had covered her hair with a bandanna and donned bright yellow rubber gloves and an old blue maternity shirt. She'd been scrubbing walls for over an hour. The ammonia in the cleaner made her nose itch; she was sure she'd rubbed it a few times, which probably meant black smudges on her face....

Josh, meanwhile, had stepped out of his bandbox again, presenting his usual bone-melting, all-male image that wedged her breath in her throat and sent desire spiraling through her. His pristine white shirt strained across his broad shoulders and muscular chest. Tailored dark slacks accented his narrow hips and hugged his long, powerful legs.

His honey-gold hair fell thick and soft over his forehead. Those turquoise eyes seared her, as always, with sensual fire. Although it was only midafternoon, a faint dark shadow already covered his firm jaw. Some primitive feminine part of her immediately conjured thoughts of that short stubble abrading her skin in certain sensitive areas. Mmm.

Oh, yes, the man was sinfully gorgeous. And unlike young Jimmy, Josh's insides, his character, matched his outsides. Dependable, sweet, thoughtful, mature. His only flaw—that inadvertent messiness—was even sort of cute, the way it always surprised him....

Any woman with a pulse would fall in love with Josh

Walker. Even before they discovered the tender heart inside the deluxe male package. *The way I did.*

"Uh...where's Michael?" he asked, shifting his weight from one foot to the other.

Smiling ruefully at the reality check, Dani pointed at the open window. "Down on the patio," she said. "Napping." She'd put the playpen in a protected but visible spot, so the baby could breath fresh air and she could keep an eye on him while she worked.

You're a fool, Dani Caldwell, she told herself, watching Josh stride to the window and look out. She'd known it was time to go, even before his heart-stopping kiss in the hospital— She'd finally heard the applause and broken the embrace, to find herself shamelessly kissing the daylights out of *him!* But for the first time in her life, Dani had no backbone. Her love for Josh kept coaxing her into finding one more task to do, so she could stay one more day. She didn't want to ever leave him, she confessed silently.

And so, like a lovestruck kid, she kept hanging around, hoping for a miracle.

"I, ahem, had an unexpected visitor today," Josh told the window ledge.

When the sill refused comment, Dani reluctantly filled the silence. "Who?"

Josh turned. Emotion simmered in his turquoise eyes, but she couldn't identify it. Then something shuttered his gaze as he took a deep breath and pushed out a flood of words in a rapid monotone. "Guy named Delbert Graves. He's a private investigator, hired by your in-laws. He traced you to Virginia through me. Graves said the Caldwells have decided not to seek custody of Michael, but talk is cheap. I feel responsible and I was thinking—"

He shoved his hands deep into his trouser pockets and turned back to address the window. "The only way to be sure you keep Michael is for us to get married, then I can adopt him legally. I'll take good care of you, Dani. Both of you. And you'll be safe forever. What do you say?''

For a moment she couldn't speak. Couldn't breathe.

"I—I don't know what to say," Dani replied finally, climbing down from the chair just as her legs gave out. She sank onto the seat and closed her eyes.

"Say yes."

"It's not that easy," she retorted, then bit her lip. *Not easy at all.* She wasn't even sure why she was hesitating. She loved Josh and he'd just asked her to marry him. It was a dream come true.

That's why.

Because it was *her* dream, not his. She loved Josh too much to chance her dream becoming his nightmare. And he *didn't say anything about loving me,* she realized. He said he felt *responsible.*

Well, that made her decision simple. A no-brainer, in fact.

She had to leave. Now, before her dreams and her heart convinced her to ignore reality. She didn't want, couldn't afford, another marriage based on fantasy and hope. She knew that was a recipe for heartbreak.

And it wasn't fair to Josh.

After all the pain he'd suffered, he deserved a chance to find a woman he could love, to have his own family. Tears stung as an image of Josh surrounded by blond-haired, blue-eyed children danced behind her eyelids.

"What's so hard about it?" he asked with a cool shrug.

Giving you up. Saying goodbye to my heart's dearest dream. Not blurting out that I love you.

She knew Josh by now. He'd do his granite-jaw thing and scowl, then insist of course he loved her, he'd just forgotten to mention it.

And he'd tiptoe around for the next forty or fifty years, treating her with careful respect and courtesy, all the time dying inside, like a plant trying to live without sunlight or water.

She couldn't allow her gentle warrior to suffer that slow, withering death.... "I can't do it," she said quickly before her selfish heart could have its way and say *yes, yes, yes.*

"Why the hell not?" he stormed—granite jaw glaringly in evidence.

What to say? Anything close to the truth would leave her open for debate and she was already weakening. Even five more minutes of temptation and she'd condemn Josh to a lifetime of the worst kind of pressure. Oh, she'd keep him satisfied in bed—the explosive kisses they'd shared made that clear—and she'd make a home for him and gladly have and raise his children, but... Deep inside, she'd want more from him than he could give.

And he'd sense it.

They'd both end up unhappy. And growing up in that atmosphere would affect the children, too.

So cut the cord quickly.

"Because I've got my own life to live, Josh." She raised her chin and tried to look convincing. "And marriage isn't in my plans...at least, not...right now...." *Wimp.*

"Well, right now's when you need it," he snapped. "If your in-laws know where I work, they know where I live, so you'd—"

"Better go," Dani finished, then closed her eyes against the raw pain that sliced through her heart as she uttered the most difficult three words she'd ever said, "I'll leave today." It felt fatal, even though she knew she wouldn't die. She couldn't.

She had a child to raise. Alone. More alone than she'd ever thought possible.

"No! You can't!" Josh looked around wildly for inspiration. He knew he'd never get her back if he let her go now. He had to stall her till he thought of something. A better argument. More leverage. Something.

"I must."

Before he could launch a nervous-babble storm designed

to hold her until his brain started working again, the phone rang. "Wait here," he ordered, and ran downstairs to snatch up the receiver.

"What?" he barked.

"Chill, Walker," Marletta advised. "Sorry to interrupt, but you're expected in Reinholdt's court—now," Marletta announced. "He's ready to rule."

"Damned despot!"

"Not engaged yet, eh?" Marletta asked.

"Not even close."

"Well, the fat lady hasn't sung yet," the secretary drawled. "Good luck—but get going. You know Reinholdt. He'll slap you with contempt faster than a politician can spew a sound bite. You'll have a heap o' trouble courting your Dani from jail."

With a grumble of agreement, Josh hung up. "I've got to go. I'm supposed to be in court in ten minutes," he reported to Dani, who'd followed him downstairs. "Don't go anywhere until I get back," he commanded, striding to the door. "Please, I mean. Just— We'll work something out, okay?"

Without waiting for an answer, he disappeared at a run.

For a moment Dani thought she might die beneath the twin tidal waves of longing and sorrow that crashed over her.

But she heard Michael fussing on the patio, reminding her that she couldn't crumple to the floor and weep for days because the man she loved had proposed marriage, but...*he doesn't love me.*

Her maternal drive kicked in, followed by survival instinct—while she fed Michael, Dani stirred up a little motivating anger.

Did Josh really think she'd just sit here like a bump on a log until he got back and "worked something out"? Big idiot.

You'll be a bigger one if you do it.

So, after burping her son, Dani packed their personal belongings and called the bus station. Lucky her—a bus left for Little Rock in an hour. From there, she could transfer to a route that would take her to Lufkin. Dani reserved a ticket.

It was time, not only to leave Virginia and Josh Walker, but to go home to Texas. To make what peace she could with Jimmy's parents. She and the Caldwells had exhibited the same grief and guilt—they'd just done so in different ways. The older couple should share what future they had left with their son's baby. Because they *were* Michael's grandparents.

And she might as well live her hollow life in Texas, among friends.

And she'd better get started.

She had enough money for bus fare, but how long would it take to get a taxi out here to take her to the bus station?

What if it didn't arrive before Josh got back? She didn't trust herself to resist him and her heart a second time.

After chewing on her lip for a minute Dani went upstairs and located Senator Perrodeaux's business card. Quickly, before she chickened out, she dialed the number written on the back.

"Senator Perrodeaux? This is Dani Caldwell. Do you remember me?…Yes, it was a wonderful evening. Yes, he's fine. Sleeping almost six hours at night now…."

Tears blurred the room around her. It was no good. Anger didn't hold back the hurt for long. She loved Josh, wanted a life with him, but to make her dream come true, she'd have to destroy his chances of happiness.

Which made the hardest thing she'd ever had to do too simple to avoid.

Taking a deep breath, Dani made the only honorable move left to her. "I wonder, sir, if you could do me a small favor…."

* * *

Josh tried not to fidget while Reinholdt droned on. He didn't bother listening. Hell, let the defendant's attorney do that.

He was busy racking his brain for something convincing to say when he got home, something to add, something he'd left out....

Tangibles, you idiot. Josh smacked his forehead. Ignored the odd looks he got from the judge and the others in the courtroom.

And not just durable consumer goods like cars and houses.

Romantic tangibles.

Proposal-of-marriage tangibles.

Josh sneaked a peek at his watch. Damn, it was getting late. *Wrap it up, would ya?* he silently begged Judge Reinholdt. *I've got to buy some flowers—lots of flowers.*

And a ring. *Yeah! That'll show her I'm serious.*

Hmm. Wonder if she'd prefer a traditional wedding ring set or an emerald to match her eyes and a gold band wide enough to be seen a block away?

He'd take her to dinner, he decided. Someplace quiet, elegant, intimate. Maybe he'd try one of those schmaltzy routines where the waitstaff conspires to hide the ring in her dessert.

Better make it the appetizer. If they got engaged tonight, they could marry tomorrow.

A flicker of panic flared through his insides. She'd turned him down once. Said she was leaving. What if she was already gone? Lord knows, Dani Caldwell was the kind of woman who waded right in and took action when she thought it needed taking...

His Honor continued to drone. Josh groaned. He had to get out of here!

He thrust his hand into his pants pocket, curled his fingers around the ignition key—

The car. "Oh, you genius you," Josh muttered, relaxing

tense muscles. No need to burn judicial bridges by yelling at Reinholdt to cut to the chase. Dani would still be there when he got home. Cabs take hours to show up in suburbs like Fallsboro, he thought with a smile at his accidental brilliance. Besides, she couldn't possibly get the playpen, the crib and all the rest of Michael's stuff packed before he got—

Suddenly his client was smiling and pumping his hand. We won. Josh rushed through the congratulations, declined an invitation to celebrate their victory and sprinted for the car.

Gunning the engine, he cut off a bailiff leaving the parking lot. The court employee honked. Josh waved.

Now, back to the ring. No diamond could match the fire and sparkle of Dani's green eyes, of course, but it was a romantic gesture with a clear meaning. Something she couldn't misunderstand.

Mechanically jiggling Michael to quiet him, Dani was able to smile and wave goodbye to the senator as his limousine pulled away from the curb. Using sheer willpower, she managed to march into the bus station and stand in the ticket line. She even managed to say, "Little Rock, please," when the clerk asked where she was going.

But Michael fell asleep while they waited for the departure announcement and so, left alone in a crowd of strangers, she dissolved into tears as she joined the line to board the silver and blue bus.

"Oh, my. Those look like heartbroke tears," said the elderly woman next to her as they shuffled forward.

Dani nodded.

"You want to talk about it?" the woman asked as they climbed into the bus and took adjoining seats.

"No, ma'am," Dani said, trying without success to smile or at least stop crying. "Thanks for your concern, but... there's nothing to say."

The woman nodded, accepting the assessment. "Well, I'm sure sorry, honey," she said, reaching over to pat Dani's hand. "But you're so young—your heart will mend before you know it and you'll fall in love again."

The bus began to pull out of the terminal and Dani took the opportunity to break off the conversation by turning her face toward the window next to her, as if to watch the scenery slide away.

Her fellow passenger meant well—and maybe she was right. In two or three centuries she might be able to look at another man. Some guy without golden hair and turquoise eyes, without a jaw that could turn to granite in the flick of an eye, whose kisses didn't melt her skeleton and sear her soul.... The scenery blurred as more tears slipped down her cheeks.

Get used to it, she told herself, shifting Michael's carrier in her lap. *It's going to take an ocean of tears to wash away your love for Josh Walker.*

Once more, Josh burst into the house.

This time, his arms were loaded with every rose in the county.

His pocket held a small, velvet box. He'd ended up just asking the jeweler for something flawless and exquisitely set; if she didn't like it, they'd exchanged the damned thing for whatever made her happy.

"Dani!" he called, one foot on the first stair.

Silence.

"Dani, where are you?"

More silence. Awful, complete, *empty* silence.

Panic started bubbling up like water in an artesian well.

"No, God. Please." Josh rushed upstairs, through the house, out the back, checked the garage. "Where the hell is she?" he muttered against his raging fear.

Finally he noticed the small rectangle tucked under the telephone in the living room. Roses slid unnoticed from his arms as he picked it up and read the number scrawled on it in expensive ink.

Josh gave it one last shot, but his fear turned to despair and swamped him like a monsoon capsizing a fishing boat when Perrodeaux's aide confirmed the senator had received a call from a young lady this afternoon and unexpectedly cleared a meeting off his schedule.

She didn't come back.

For twenty-four straight hours Josh sat at the foot of the stairs, watching the front door. Waiting. Then he tightened his jaw, stumbled into the living room and tried to work. He needed five pages of tightly written, exhaustively documented, well-reasoned argument for some damned "important" brief he had to file…oh, sometime.

He had three sentences. Only one of which had both a subject and a verb. "The hell with it," he growled, and threw the yellow legal pad across the room.

The hell with the Supreme Court. The hell with everything.

Josh rubbed a hand tiredly over his eyes. He still couldn't believe it. He still didn't know how she could leave him like that. She wasn't Carrie, with some weird agenda of her own.

It was him. This one was his fault—one hundred percent.

And now he understood what Dani had tried to show him. Taking responsibility, fixing blame, *forgiving* didn't change anything.

She was gone. They were gone. Dani and Michael. His family.

And he was never getting over them. Never.

He'd lost his last chance at a baby. Last chance at happiness. Last chance at love.

And it hurt. Too much to stuff away. Too much to freeze out. Too much, maybe, even to survive….

An evening's soft dusky light was shifting through the windows when Marletta walked in uninvited. She stood in the archway between foyer and living room with her hands on her hips. Gazing at the rubble of his life. Frowning.

"So this is where you've been hiding," she said finally with a disdainful snort. "Walker," she continued, striding toward him, "you're pathetic."

Chapter Ten

After looking around—for the first time in days, apparently—Josh supposed he was pathetic. Roses, wilted and brown, lay scattered on the floor where he'd dropped them. A pizza box and a couple of Chinese take-out cartons sat on the coffee table, so he must have eaten. He rubbed a hand over his jaw. He hadn't shaved in a while. Had he slept?

He couldn't remember. All he knew was that the pain hadn't gone away, hadn't eased a bit.

"Did it occur to you to at least call in and let me know you were staying home to wallow in self-pity?" Marletta echoed his sister-in-law's condemnation with a snarl in her voice.

"Sorry," he said with a sigh.

"You sure are, Walker." She pivoted on her heel and headed for the door. "And by the way, I quit."

"Huh?" Dimly, Josh realized his work was all he had now—and without Marletta Langtry, he might as well close his doors. "You can't do that," he protested weakly.

Marletta turned around. Pointed a finger at him. "I can

and I will," she retorted, "if you don't snap out of it, Walker. I'll move to Los Angeles. My second oldest runs a body shop there. Or maybe I'll—"

"Dammit, she left!" Josh sat forward and thrust his fingers through his hair. "What am I supposed to do?"

"Go after her, you fool."

Josh knew she wanted him to fight back. But he couldn't. He was paralyzed by the pain of losing Dani. And his baby.

"And do what when I find her?" he asked wearily. "If I *could* find her...."

"How should I know?" the secretary snapped. "Just don't sit there dying inside and let her go."

"What more can I do?" Josh spread his hands helplessly. "I asked her to marry me. She refused."

"Why?"

"How should I know? Because she didn't want to marry me, I guess."

"You *guess?*" The hair on the back of his neck rose at Marletta's tone. "What in the name of heaven is wrong with you, Walker? I saw the way she looked at you that night you went to dinner with the senator. She was in love with you then. What did you do to change her mind?"

Josh suddenly knew how badgered witnesses felt. "Nothing," he said with a defensive shrug. "She said she couldn't marry me. She had her own life to live."

"What the heck does that mean?"

"I don't know!" he shouted desperately, leaping to his feet. "Look, after I got rid of Graves, I came home, explained that he'd located her and told her we should get married. That way, I could adopt Michael and she wouldn't have to worry if the Caldwells sued for custody. Then she—"

He stopped in midsentence. Marletta seemed to be having some kind of attack. Her eyes bulged. She sputtered, apparently having difficulty breathing.

Well, that released him from the lethargy of hopelessness

that had held him prisoner of the sofa for the past four or five days! Josh raced to her side. "What is it?" he cried. "Should I call 9-1-1?"

Marletta shook her head, then bent forward and put her hand over her heart as she—

"You're...*laughing?*" Josh asked in astonishment. "What the hell is so funny?"

"Y-you are, Walker. For a brilliant lawyer, known for his silver-tongued oratory in court, you take the—" Gales of laughter burst from the secretary again. When she finally regained a semblance of control, she asked him, "Did you bother to tell Dani that you love and adore her?"

"We never talked about love!" Josh retorted, then closed his eyes as the full extent of his stupidity sank in. "Oh, sh—" He clapped his hand against his forehead. "I didn't... But couldn't she— She doesn't know..."

He spread his hands wide as he appealed to his secretary's superior wisdom. "Do you think I stand a chance if I throw myself at her feet and declare undying love?"

"Might be a start," Marletta said with a grin. "'Course you ought to follow that with some concrete proof. Like, a ring or...."

Josh rummaged around until he found the velvet box. Showed his secretary—and savior—the diamond solitaire set in a band of baguettes. "A ring like this, you mean?"

Marletta whistled silently, then nodded.

"But...how am I going to find her?" he asked with a frown. "It's a big country—she could be anywhere!"

"If she loves you," Marletta assured him, "she won't be that hard to find." She pulled the ubiquitous pencil from her hair and produced a notepad from her purse. "Now, let's get you organized to make that declaration."

As they conferred, Josh thought that if Congress *really* wanted a balanced budget or social programs that actually worked, they'd hire Marletta Langtry and let her red pencil loose.

Within minutes they'd formulated a plan and plunged into action. Marletta made a list of appointments to reschedule while Josh contacted Senator Perrodeaux and studied the atlas. Reaching a mutual conclusion, they considered calling the Caldwells—telephoned Delbert Graves instead. Then Josh raced upstairs to shower, shave and change.

He scooped up some additional clothes, threw them in a bag and headed for the airport.

Boarded the next appropriate plane, which deposited him in Houston, where he rented a car and drove north on a red asphalt highway cutting its way into the green, forested heart of East Texas.

Beautiful country, Josh thought idly as the car ate miles. If Dani wanted to move back to Lufkin, he'd agree in a heartbeat. With faxes and E-mail, he could office anywhere; when he needed to make personal appearances, Houston had two airports and so did Dallas. What was a few hours' drive compared to her happiness? And his.

Whatever Dani wanted, she'd get—as long as she'd take him, too.

The address Graves had given him belonged to a rambling, redbrick fifties-style ranch house, set way back from a wide, tree-lined street. Josh pulled into the drive, cut the engine and got out. Walked to the front door and rang the doorbell, torn between hope and hostility.

A beefy, middle-aged man with salt-and-pepper hair, sun-leathered skin and hands that had done plenty of physical labor opened the door. "Can I help you?" he asked with a drawl so like Dani's that Josh felt homesick.

He shook it off and said in a carefully neutral voice, "I'm looking for Pete Caldwell."

"You found him," the man conceded without releasing his grip on the door. "What can I do for you?"

Josh hesitated. He'd spent the plane trip devising various approaches for this meeting, depending on the amount of resistance he encountered—but he couldn't get a reading on this man to know which one to take.

Might as well keep it simple, then. "My name's Walker," he said. "Josh Walker. And the reason I—"

He broke off in midsentence because he heard a familiar sound coming from the back of the house. The sound of a baby crying. And not just any baby, dammit.

"Where is he?" Josh demanded, pushing his way into the house. "Where's Michael?"

The older man indicated a doorway at the far end of the room. "In the kitchen. I take it you've met my grandson?"

With a curt nod, Josh headed in the direction Caldwell pointed. The kitchen contained the usual appliances—in harvest gold—and an Early American dinette set. A shelf ran around three walls of the room near the ceiling, every inch of it filled with commemorative plates and china poodles. In the center of the room stood a short, round woman with brown hair and eyes. Trying to get Michael to take a bottle. The poor darling baby, whose little face was streaked with tears, spit out the nipple and turned his head away.

Josh reached her in one stride. "Come here, precious," he crooned as he lifted Michael from her and cradled him against his own chest. Once the baby was secure, he prepared to lash out at the cruel, brown-haired woman. "Aside from the fact that he's lactose intolerant—" he began, only to be cut off.

"So was his father, young man," she snapped. "This is a soy product designed for that very problem and he's been doing fine on it."

"Then he's not hungry," Josh declared while the baby snuggled closer. "He's tired."

"Well, that's what I thought, but he kept on crying when I rocked him. I couldn't think of what to do." The woman smiled sheepishly. "To tell the truth, it's been so long since I had a baby this small that I've forgotten most of what I knew—and how much work they are."

"He only likes to be rocked at night. Naptimes, he likes this—'' Josh demonstrated the pat-circle, pat-circle stroke he'd discovered. Sure enough, within a few moments, Michael hiccuped, stopped crying and yawned against Josh's neck.

Pete Caldwell had followed Josh to the kitchen. Now he crossed the room to stand behind his wife, resting his hands protectively on her shoulders. "We appreciate the advice, Mr. Walker, but maybe you'd better explain why you're here."

"I'm looking for Dani," he declared, glaring at the older couple over Michael's back. "Where is she? If you think you can just grab this child without a fight, you're sadly mistaken. Kidnapping is a federal offense—"

"Hold on, son," Pete Caldwell said quietly, raising one hand and holding it palm outward. "I think there's been a mistake—"

"You can say that again, buddy," Josh snarled.

Caldwell squeezed his wife's shoulders. "Looks like you were right, Edna," he said, chuckling. "There's a little more between these two than good Samaritanism."

He turned his attention back to Josh. "That baby you're holding so expertly is our grandson and we intend to be a part of his life, young man, but we've no desire to have custody of Michael full-time."

"Then why did you threaten Dani with—"

Edna interrupted him. "That was grief talking, Mr. Walker. I don't know if you can understand how—" The woman paused to wipe tears from her eyes.

"How much it hurts?" Josh asked softly. "Yes, ma'am, I do."

"Well," Edna went on more briskly, "the past couple of days reminded us why kids need to be raised by young folks. We're too old to do this full-time!"

"Michael needs grandparents, too," Josh assured her. "But—where's Dani?"

"It was plain as dirt that she had a lot on her mind when she came back from Virginia," Pete Caldwell said, eyes narrowed now. "Wouldn't talk about nothin', though. Once we got the air cleared between us, she accepted our offer to watch Michael for a couple of days so's she could think things through."

"What things?" Josh wanted to know. Needed to know. Had she already dismissed him from her life or was there another second chance for him? "No, wait—don't tell me." He would give the past value by using what he'd learned from it. "Let me ask *Dani* that question. Do you know where she is now?"

Pete Caldwell studied Josh for a long moment. "Not exactly," he offered finally. "She's been checking in with us. But she said if we needed to get a message to her, we should call a Dr. Ravjani in No Lake and he'd send word out to the cabin, wherever that is."

Josh forced himself to keep patting Michael's back; he wanted to jump and shout and twirl Edna around until they were both dizzy. "Mr. Caldwell, I'm going to ask you a very important question. How would you feel about somebody helping Dani raise Michael? Somebody who's probably going to make plenty of mistakes along the way, but who loves your grandson—and his mother—more than life itself."

The Caldwells communed silently for a few seconds, then— "Mistakes make us human, son. I made some I'll always regret…" Pete said. "But the pain of losin' Jimmy has taught me one thing—in the end, love is all that matters."

Michael's grandfather held out his hand. "Welcome to the family."

Josh carefully transferred the now-sleeping Michael to Edna's arms, then shook Pete's hand.

Then he got the hell out of there.

Drove due west for about six hours. Found San Angelo

this time. Rented a motel room long enough to sleep a little, then shower and shave. Pulled on jeans, his lucky chambray shirt and his boots. Wolfed down a fast-food breakfast, bought some buckets to set behind the car's front seat, filled them with water and all the roses he could find.

Then, settling back against the upholstery, Josh slipped sunglasses on against the bright Texas morning and headed west again.

As he drove, Josh prayed that he'd been through hell for the last time this lifetime....

Though the chilly predawn and the spectacular purple, gold and magenta of sunrise had long since given way to bright sunlight and burgeoning heat, Dani remained seated on the rocky ledge behind the cabin, looking out over the desert, willing its deep, eternal silence to seep into her soul, to ease the pain of missing Josh.

It didn't work this time, either, so she uncrossed her legs with a sigh and prepared to leave her perch. Time to go back inside and pretend again to work on her lists of menus, cost estimates and marketing ideas.

When she'd mentioned her plan to supply home-cooked meals to people with no time to cook, Pete Caldwell had insisted on providing the start-up money. She'd accepted his offer because—brokenhearted or not—she had a child to raise. Although he refused to sign formal loan papers, Dani wanted to show him some facts and figures when she returned tomorrow to get Michael.

She'd called the Caldwells from Little Rock and they'd met the bus when it arrived in Lufkin. They'd had a long talk and shed a few tears together and although their relationship was still fragile, Dani believed the Caldwells' desire to reconcile with her and their grandson was sincere.

That's why she'd returned to Texas, why she'd agreed to let them keep Michael while she gathered her thoughts and prepared to cope with the rest of her life.

Oh, be honest. She'd hightailed it back to the Lone Star State to avoid temptation. Only by putting a thousand miles or so between her and Josh Walker could she be sure her heart wouldn't overrule her head and ask him to renew his offer.

A tear trickled down her cheek. She closed her eyes, trying to hold the rest back. She'd cried enough already and not one of those tears had changed the facts.

She loved Josh, but he didn't love her.

Are you sure? whispered her foolish heart. *And even if he doesn't, he asked you to marry him. Wanted to adopt Michael...*

This was no boy proposing on a whim, making promises he didn't know if he could keep.

Josh Walker was a man. Tried, tested...*and true.*

Can you say the same for yourself?

Even if she'd done the right thing, Dani realized as she plodded back to the cabin to escape the glare of the desert sun, she'd done it the wrong way. Carrie's way.

He'd asked her to wait, to work something out—and she'd just walked away without a word. "Not even a thank-you," she muttered as she rounded the corner of the cabin and climbed the porch.

She owed him that, at least. And not just for standing by her all these weeks and caring for Michael. Josh had helped her overcome her reluctance to dream again, to try again. To risk love again.

True, her heart was broken—but she'd known real, adult, lasting love.

If she fell short of achieving her career goals, too, well...at least, she'd given it a shot. Failing was more of a success than never trying at all.

Dani curled her hand around the doorknob. "Okay," she promised, "I'll write him a let—"

"Help!"

A shiver ran down her spine at the faint cry. Was that a real voice or her imagination? It sounded like—

"Help! Help!"

"Hold on!" she whispered as her heart began pounding. "Oh, hold on…"

Then Dani was sprinting down the path that led from the cabin to the highway. Risking her neck as her feet slipped on the loose pebbles, but it didn't matter. Nothing mattered because…

"Help me!"

She skidded around the big boulder at the bend in the path, grabbed its rocky curve to halt her progress. And stared.

It *was* him.

Her dear, crazy, handsome, gruff, tender, darling Josh Walker stood on her boulder's twin, out in the dry streambed—his arms filled with roses.

"Help," he said quietly, that lopsided grin echoing the uncertainty she could see—even this far away—in his beautiful turquoise eyes. "You've got to help me, Dani," he declared, and jumped down from the boulder with his armload of roses.

Stunned by the intensity of her desire to hurl herself into his embrace and spin away to heaven with his kiss, her voice was unsteady as she asked, "How… Wh-what kind of help do you need?"

"I need another second chance, Dani." He took one step toward her. "And only you can give it to me."

The Queen of Coping couldn't manage anything more intelligent than, "Huh?"

"When you pulled me out of that arroyo during that flash flood—" Josh held the mass of roses, already drooping in the desert heat, against his massive chest "—you gave me a second chance to live. Now I'm asking for a second chance to propose."

"Josh, I…" Nervously she brushed loose curls away

from her face as selfless love and selfish desire warred inside her.

"Please," he said raggedly, closing the distance between them. "If you turn me down, I'll—" He shook his head and somehow did that granite jaw thing while flashing a wry, sexy, *irresistible* smile.

And Dani didn't want to resist any longer. *Why not take what he offers and love him for the rest of your life?* she asked herself. Maybe, sometime in the future, he'll—

"No, I won't promise to go away, Dani," Josh said, his deep voice melting the very last of her resistance. "I can't. Marry me, Dani, please. I love you. Maybe I don't know how to express it, but I'll learn. You can teach me, like you teach Michael."

Dani couldn't believe her ears. "Y-you love me?"

"Hell, yes," he growled, and her feet overruled her head.

Some of the roses fell into the desert dust. Some were crushed between them as she flew into his arms.

"Does that mean yes, I hope?" he asked, reveling in the feel of this woman—his woman, as soon as he could arrange it—in his arms. Where she belonged forever.

"Say it again," she commanded in a dreamy voice.

"I love you, Dani Caldwell."

"And Michael, too?"

"Oh, yes. And my—*our* darling baby Michael, too."

"Show me," she said, leaning back without breaking the embrace. He could see deep into her forest-glade eyes. Her *shadowless* forest-glade eyes, brimming with love and desire. "Take me up to the cabin right now and show me how you love me, Josh."

He raised one trembling hand to capture a strand of curling maple hair. Nothing about their relationship had been "normal" since the very beginning, but Josh was determined to be traditional from now on.

"As soon as we're married," he promised, "I will show

you in every way that I love you with all my heart and all my soul.

"In the meantime—" he dug the little velvet box out of his pocket and pried it open "—let this symbolize my love."

Josh jerked the ring free of its box, which he dropped into the arroyo's dust along with a leftover rose or two. Carefully, he slid the solitaire into place. On Dani's third finger, left hand.

Her green eyes were warm now, like Montana pine trees caught in spring sunlight, and Josh gathered her close. She nestled her cheek against his chest.

"I don't expect you to love me back, Dani. Not ye—"

She touched a finger to his lips. "I do love you, Josh," she assured him, "and I'll marry you as soon as the law allows."

He couldn't help it. He picked her up and twirled her around until they were both laughing and dizzy. Because Dani had just turned his empty, sterile existence into a lifetime of passion and joy.

"What about children?" she asked when he staggered to a halt.

Josh set her down gently. He'd expected her question. In fact, he'd been prepared to raise it himself. This time, the subject would be discussed beforehand.

None of which made it easy, but Josh knew his answer came from his heart.

"We have Michael," he said, brushing his lips on the top of her head. "Being his father is all any man could ask for."

"Michael is not going to be an only child," Dani declared as her fingers stole to the top of his shirtfront. "Wouldn't you like another little boy someday?" she asked and undid the first button. "Someday *soon*," she elaborated, working on the second and third buttons. "With blond hair and blue eyes.'' Her fingers trailed liquid fire down his chest as she reached for the next button on his shirt.

Reluctantly, Josh closed his hands over her fingers. This sensual torture had to stop until they got one or two things straight. They weren't doing anything precipitate. Not this time.

They were going to wait, if it killed him—and it might.

"Green," he gasped as Dani abandoned de-buttoning in favor of kissing the skin she'd exposed. "I want a daughter with green eyes and your hair."

His hands wrapped themselves around her silky braid and tugged gently to halt her erotic exploration of his torso. "I'm not making the same mistake twice," he insisted with a groan. "We're going by the book from now on. First, we get engaged—"

"Done," Dani chimed, turning her hand to make the diamond sparkle.

"Then we get married," Josh went on doggedly, "then we go on our honeymoon. Then and *only* then do we make love. And babies."

"No."

Everything stopped. "No?" She'd changed her mind? Already? Not much of a last second chance, he thought as waves of anguish crashed over him.

Dani studied the play of emotions over his features, heard the hurt and confusion vibrating in his deep voice. Felt a flutter of feminine pride that this man, this sophisticated, successful, sexy-as-hell man needed to be assured of her love. Needed *her*. As much as she needed him.

"I mean—maybe we should skip the go-somewhere part of the honeymoon," she explained quickly, her green eyes dancing as she smiled mischievously. "Why don't we just stay home with Michael?"

Josh sighed with relief—and anticipation. Still… "Nope," he said as his lips nuzzled the satiny skin below her earlobe. "We're going to go the whole nine yards. You just name the date. I'll make all the arrangements. For once,'' he added with a rueful chuckle, ''let me handle the situation.''

Dani chewed on her lip. She couldn't possibly wait to commit her life to Josh Walker—not long enough for Mr. Messy to pull together a big wedding. But why argue? When the senator had driven her to the bus station, he'd informed her that Virginia had no waiting period, so if worse came to worst, there *was* a simple solution.

With a giggle, Dani wrapped her arms around Josh's neck. ''I'll give you a week,'' she said. ''And not a moment longer.''

Epilogue

This time, Dani stopped to smooth out a fold in the skirt of the organza and lace creation hanging on the closet door. Then—she couldn't help herself—she patted the cloud of tulle gathered into a pearl-studded headdress that hung atop the gown.

"It *is* a beautiful dress, isn't it?" she whispered as she forced herself away from its exquisiteness. Just a few more hours now and she could put it on. Climb into the limo and be driven to the church.

Where she and Josh—

"Ahbeege."

And Michael. And one or two more children. Soon, if they were lucky. We are, Dani thought with a laugh as she lifted the baby from his playpen and kissed his cheek. Lucky child. *Lucky me.*

"Ahglooo."

"I agree, tiger," Josh said from the stairway, where he stood with a suitcase in each hand.

Automatically shifting Michael's weight against her hip, Dani smiled up at her very-soon-to-be husband.

Because he'd done it. Just as he'd promised.

After feverishly studying every bridal magazine and book in the D.C. area, Josh had hired a wedding consultant, two florists, a travel agent, and a caterer, then recruited not only his secretary but Senator Perrodeaux, too.

Together, they'd pulled it off. One week after that second proposal, a flawlessly orchestrated and thoroughly traditional wedding was about to commence.

So traditional that Josh had insisted on moving out of the house until they were married because, he said, he didn't trust himself to stop at courtship kisses and he was determined to wait until their wedding night.

He'd stopped by the town house this morning only to pack what he needed for the honeymoon.

Now he was headed for the airport to pick up the Caldwells, who'd agreed to give away the bride.

Which reminded her—

"Josh, are you sure you want to bring the baby on our honeymoon?" she asked. "The Caldwells said they'd be happy to keep him while we're in Florida."

"No way," Josh declared, his turquoise eyes warm as he dropped the suitcases to pluck Michael from her arms and settle the infant against his massive chest. "Our son wants a set of those mouse-ears."

Dani laughed at his fatherly foolishness, then asked softly, "And what do you want, Josh?"

"You, darling. My Texas bride. And all the children you'll give me." His slow, lopsided smile promised a lifetime of sensual delight and husbandly devotion. "Just let me love you always the way I love you now.

"Of course, if you'd like a technical suggestion..." He leaned toward her.

Dani closed her eyes as he whispered in her ear. Oh, yes, she would definitely fulfill that fantasy— *"You above me, your glorious hair tumbling loose, brushing over me...."*

It was only fair. Josh had already fulfilled *her* dreams.

Lasting love. A home and family. A happily ever after they'd share for a lifetime.

Josh's mouth hovered above hers. Dani lifted her head, eager to receive one of his bone-melting kisses. She'd missed him so much this wee—

"Get away from that woman!" Marletta yelled from the foyer. "Go wait at the church." She'd come to boss, er, help the bride dress.

Obediently, Josh handed over Michael, picked up his suitcases, and loped downstairs. As he headed through the front door, he paused. "Oh, uh, Dani?"

"Mmm..." With difficulty, she dragged her thoughts back to the present from the almost-here future of her wedding night with the most wonderful man on earth. "What, darling?"

"Don't, ah, don't go in the master bedroom, okay? I'll, uh, I swear—I'll straighten it up when we get back."

*   *   *   *   *

"Josh, are you sure—" Dani resisted, pressing the baby on her shoulder—the infant's sleep could be delicate enough to be lost if so much as a whisper were to intrude. "Shhh."

"No, no." Josh clasped Mr. Importer Guy's arm as he dropped the suitcases beside Michael's crib. "Don't be silly. He's the man against the one—or Chuck? Oh, you won't be in of it at all—"

Dani listened to her husband's confidence, silent, and at odds with it. "And love me, really am, Josh?"

Then, turning, Mrs. Tracy Bride, said all the children you'll give me?" He slow regarded a life he needed a life hard to restrain thinking, and he gently drew sent. "Now, I'm...love you, always, maybe I love you, yes?"

Of course so, with a Dani, he almost suggested. He handed over her.

Dani closed her eyes as he whispered in her ear. Oh, yes, Dani could definitely think that fantasy! The cruise, me two, stones—they'd been living for a breathe, even after. It was amly full, Josh had already fulfilled her. Perhaps

If you enjoyed what you just read,
then we've got an offer you can't resist!

Take 2 bestselling love stories FREE!

Plus get a FREE surprise gift!

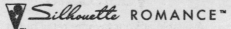